Wall of Darkness

by *J. Lea Koretsky*

Best Wishes

[signature]

REGENT PRESS

Library of Congress Cataloging-in-Publication Data

Koretsky, Judy Lea.
    Wall of darkness / by J. Lea Koretsky.
        p.cm.
    ISBN 1-58790-020-3
        1. Women journalists--Fiction. 2. Female friendship--Fiction.
3. Pedophilia--Fiction. 4. Internet--Fiction. 5. Hawaii--Fiction.
I. Title.

PS3611.074 W35 2002
813'.6--dc21   2002069970

Manufactured in the U.S.A.

REGENT PRESS
6020-A Adeline Street
Oakland, CA 94608
regentpress@mindspring.com

"How bad is it?" I asked, as we climbed into the bucket seats and started off.

"Awful." A cigarette burned in the ashtray. She picked it up and jamming it into her mouth, she cut across three lanes, narrowly missing drivers, and sped to the highway. "I spent most of the night looking at photographs. This is a boy. He's dead. He's a kid, a nice looking suburban youngster whose parents are probably frantic trying to decide where he is and why they haven't heard from him."

"How is he related to this teenager you were describing?"

"He was seen with him hours before the body was found."

I was quiet. I wasn't the type to go to pieces over a disgusting homicide scene and neither was she. We had tromped through grassy villages and slept beneath palm trees and listened to gunfire on and off throughout the nights we were in Cambodia and then had encountered dead children slaughtered by gunfire. In the black and white photos Libby had taken the scrawny bodies and tumbled graves spoke as loudly as the look of fear stamped into their stoop of shoulder, body shielding body, hands covering the faces of children and infants. The war was a mess and I had learned much that spring about keeping my voice quiet about things I wasn't supposed to know, or see.

Out of heartfelt gratitude I would like to thank those people who contributed support to me during the writing of this novel. They are Mystery Writers of America, the Tuesday lunch group, San Francisco Medical Examiner Boyd Stephens, Administration of Justice Professor David Levesey, Richard Bradburn, the Juvenile Division of the Concord Police, Keith Inman for his class on forensic DNA, Dr. Mindy Rosenberg for her insights into crimes against children, Dr. Anne Graffam Walker Forensic Linguist for her contributions to language skills of traumatized children, to the Captain Zodiac Raft Expedition of Kauai, to my writing mentor and coach for three years Dr. James Frey, for the untiring perseverence of my friend who is in the Coast Guard who wishes to remain nameless, for Mark Weiman at Regent Press, my sister Rachel Beth and my brothers Milo David and Morey Daniel, my coworkers at Contra Costa Children's Protective Services, Shawn C. Turner for his gifted artwork and last but not least my new friends - Christie Kelly, Janet and Al Bonner, Barbara Bowers, Kay Gorman, Helen Martin, Dawn Rose, Dorothy Sandelius, the Thompsons, the Trujillos and Minister Sean Parker Dennison - for their kindness and shared wisdom.

for my mother

one

I HAD COME to Hawaii to write an article on the sovereignty movement. I had long been an admirer of traditionalist lifestyles, myself a conservative although tolerant agnostic, and coming to the realization at age forty-six that some palatte of spirituality was necessary to quiet the aching heart, I naturally gravitated to American cultures that drew their mythology from a concept of harvest and plenty. With its Meneheune cultural remnants and fishing ponds which allowed for small fish to swim through concrete grates into a large pond where they fed until they were large enough to be trapped, I looked to those aspects of the Hawaiian past that could contain guideposts to a middle aged woman seeking her own pond without also being trapped by it.

Sovereignty, I suppose, is one of those ideas that raises eyebrows by its very nature because it severely challenges the concept of democracy. There is no substitute for freedom. Royalty however need not pose a restriction. Certainly the British and indeed recently defrocked kingdoms have come to the opinion that to feed the masses involves an industrialist if not paternalistic society made up of companies and agencies that provide economy as well as governance. But Hawaii up to the 1890s was ruled by a queen and her subjects were fierce loyalists who might have been offended by the mainlander's curious attitude that a senate and assembly encourages difference whereas a royal house does not.

If Hawaii's acceptance of Brigham Young's teachings bent her to the disposition she was to be conquered by the United States military, then a less than amicable force, her education system and initial lack of crime suggested that a society ruled by a queen in several ways outstripped gains created by statehood. Hawaii had after all withstood hundreds of years of attempts to conquer her by aggressive lineages of succession and attempts to cultivate her as a protectorate. By the time military leaders walked onto her shores she had developed healthy spawning pools, matched not even by modern-day fisheries; she had an equitable education system which taught boys and girls about an egalitarian culture, and the incidence of crime including child endangerment, theft, felonious assault and homicide were virtually unheard of. Molestation also, rewarded by throwing the offender over a cliff to his death, was also a rarity.

As a journalist writing on staff for a busy city desk I may have nursed contemplations that women should be equal to men in all obligations of social institutions and looked with disdain at those corporations trodding into the twenty-first century which were still in their hierarchies male dominated and male favored by way of salaries and promotions. And although I was aware that in Hawaii on all her islands to accomodate the cost of living a family had to have two adults who each worked one and a half jobs, I was also cognizant of the fact there were proportionately a larger segment of women leaders in almost every walk of life. Their medical system also was preventive and continued to rank low in surgery and invasive treatments.

My associates spared me lectures on spicy and high fat foods although they sent me on my way with a stack of brochures on myths and history. The City of Refuge which protected the culture at large from criminals who either were ostracized or had fled death was marked in felt tip pen on my map of places to see. So was the wilderness area near a live volcano and a day trip down a steep ravine to the leper colony of the past to which the British in their wisdom sent these unfortunate disease-ravaged wanderers. If I had time between interviews with activists, the docent of a cultural museum on the Big Island and an educator whose mother had taught during the days when the Queen ruled and island hopping, I scribled a note to myself to travel to Queen's Bath and to the hydroelectricity plant for comparison impressions.

Instinctively as the plane veered toward the island of Oahu and we flew above crystaline waters and a white sandy beach inhabited by a good two hundred tourists, I hugged the pack containing my Minolta camera and tape recorder to my side patting it to make certain I was ready to snap a few rolls of film as I disembarked. The urge to capture what the eye readily takes in uncensored is a blessing for any journalist and my need for immediacy was heightened because of it. I unzipped the pouch and readied the camera lens, then glanced at the passengers who were already unbidden standing to collect bags from the overhead compartment with generalized anxiety. Since much of what a journalist does is semi-conscious and because it had been years since I last set foot in the islands, I would wait until the plane was nearly empty in order to give myself long, focussed wide angle shots of first impressions as I walked down the ramp into the airport.

THE DAY WAS HOT and muggy, a good hundred degree heat complicated by a stultifying windless zone. Not unlike the *hamsin winds* of Israel's summer months. A dead zone that gave rise to such profound irritation that those who were already emotionally on edge were driven to attempt suicide. I carried the pack on my back, all the while shooting pictures at everyone and everything, as I flowed with the crowd to the baggage carousel. Ahead of me a stewardess, her blond pony tail hanging limp in a yellow cloth band exercised well-formed calves as she steered through the crowd. Also the ten year old child whose family had sent her no doubt to rendezvous with a family member who had sat with another stewardess, her curly brown hair bouncing atop the child's confident head. So much of the world, I thought about the view she had of the trip across the ocean. At maturity age she would have done this trip a zillion times and would be able to read with her eyes closed.

A woman in a colorful flowery blouse and white skirt draped a lei of yellow and white gardenias around my neck and murmured something about a welcome. Recognizing the name of the newspaper on my badge she led me to the carousel for first-in-line service and heralded a cab for me. As soon as I spotted and grabbed my suitcase, I walked to the çab. He was a young man, in his late twenties, who talked the entire length of the trip about his two small children, a sister-in-law in the food transport business and the recent purchase of a two bedroom condo. He was doing better than most I surmised as the driver approached Honolulu. The skyline was congested with high rise apartments, motels and glass buildings. The mountains were as I recollected them, stark, jagged and mighty, a presence to be reckoned with in erecting highways and new tunnel passages. The passage of six years time had done little to mar the backbone that encompassed the indefatigueable city which revealed itself as a glittering facade, replete in every way, having healed itself from a world war and now having stepped into a new era where the housing real estate was competing with shortage of land for food and exports.

A thick layer of smog hung in the air. This was a reminder that air pollution had settled in as a very real threat to fields of produce and flowers and breathing air, giving tourism its priority as a double edged dollar. The Oahu I remembered was a flower paradise and as such competed for quality air along with the megabuck industries that had come to center stage, among them airplanes and wind turbines.

At the Sheraton I paid the cabbie a steep gratuity, then

saw my own entrance to the lobby and the checkin desk.

A T ONE TIME all that mattered was landing the best possible interview. It was a silliness that kept me tied to the telephone and in later years to a cell phone, tracking down that one source or piece of information that could turn a damp subject into a vibrant one. We're a hybrid breed - journalists. It goes without saying that if not for the amount of competition half of us would still remain in the industry with telephone cords tied to our necks. Reality is a cool bite that has pushed more than most to seek a stable middle class lifestyle in allied occupations such as computer programming, consulting work or stacked us in eager lines at the offices of head hunters to whom hopefuls would promise a full year's gross salary for landing a high paid job with perks.

I decided well into my thirties that if my reputation could not sell me, I'd always resemble a has-been. I opted for a clean desk, a professional appearance of being timely and thorough and over the years maintained a gallery morgue of experts in any field under the sun. This has paid off by getting me into narrow spaces with execs who had less than fifteen minutes or by flying to crime scenes or traffic panic areas with photographers and on a handful of occasions with the competition. There are secrets in this trade we swear we'll never tell and invariably do when we come to the end of our roads at age sixty or seventy and it looks as if time has stopped only at our doorstep. I spent hours on dangerous assignments shopping the neighborhood so-to-speak for other journalists who had covered some thin intangible thread one year ago or twenty years ago. After a twenty-five year career I stand among one hand of fingers who can pull on command from other desks, even when it makes little sense to do so.

I had met Libby Cramer on a remote assignment when I flew with a desk associate in 1970 to the wilds of Vietnam to interview designees fleeing Cambodian camps. She worked for the Sun, the Hawaiian newspaper located in Honolulu, and spoke fluent Chinese. The United States government was waging its own mercenary war against the North Vietnamese who for twenty years were sticking it to the South Vietnamese and for a reason no one could penetrate was running target assignments over the border of Cambodia. She was fifteen years older than I was, had a son in college whom she had a hard time communicating with and a husband in a wheelchair for arthritis and as a result of being the sole wage earner was hell bent on returning to the states with the only story anyone would ever see in print as to the hostilities in the Southeast. It was a good deal for me because I was young, relatively inexperienced in a war and didn't know whether I had the stomach for the stuff to land me in the city room. Had I gone on as I was I would've landed a routine of covering sports along with a bevvy of jocks who all knew what it was like first hand to be a guy and get kicked in the balls. Not bad for a female stick but not great either; not where the status is.

I placed a call to her office and her home after I showered, changed into cords and a lightweight blouse designed for muggy heat and snacked on mango slices and sticky rice delivered to the door by a hotel specialist. She answered on the first ring. She was picking me up first thing in the morning for a news-breaking disaster that would if uninterrupted within the next forty-eight hours destroy tourism at special sites. There had been a shooting of a businessman on Ala Moana Boulevard a week ago and the state police had turned the city upsidedown seeking the suspect who had fired the gun. The suspect was described as a teen Asian tough guy who was known to the financial district for being a pickpocket and creating disturbances in commercial buildings that housed Internet or On line technology. Six in the morning sharp, camera fully loaded, cassette recorder, notepad, pencil, ruler, evidence bags, so on and so forth. I said I'd be ready.

I called my editor in Concord, California and asked him to check on rumors around the Islands. He called me back in half an hour and said he had a laundry list. A series of infiltrations into the black market related to cybersex were hitting the streets. They involved normal adults, thought to be workaholics usually, entering chats about nude pictures of Asian girls, or late teens encouraged by windfall fantasies and living on the edge describing a new preoccupation with porn websites. He said also in Honolulu two separate cases would be heard this week on voyeur sites and Internet stalking. One case involved trading sex in chat rooms and escort services with prepubescent teens and featured a thousand children posing nude on the web; the other case involved a hidden camera observing girls in a private residence in various stages of dress. He rang off saying if Libby's case offered a story he would extend my time.

It was late afternoon. Five twenty. If I accessed any information in advance of the next day's jaunt it would be to verify the legal status of sex on the Net. I called a handful of typing pools for legal assistants through services like Kelly Girl until I found someone who would talk to me. The status of these cases had not yet been determined by the federal courts. Offenders who were convicted of stalking or child endangerment faced probationary status but not prison and subsequent parole. Without covert acts of violence such as rape, perversion, shoplifting, arachnephilia or axilism, compulsive behavior in and of itself was in a grey area. The subject was new, the issue of damage uncertain and many children made unconvincing witnesses in the face of assured males who were both substantive providers and seemingly loyal husbands.

My laptop said the etiology for sex on the Net was the men were usually young and suffering from relationship disorders such as locating a potential partner, or having distortions of feelings and being lost in fantasy, spending so much time in chat rooms that job, marriage and social life were becoming damaged. These men were spending hundreds of dollars a month, some were paying for telephone sex or anonymous sex or to exploit vulnerable or physically disabled young teens. A psychiatrist had dubbed it the Lolita trap, and I figured I should cruise the downtown by night and look up at the blocks of light on each balcony to see whether male eyes were rivetted to the windows.

But I didn't. Instead I called my contacts for the sovereignty movement and moved the interviews to afternoon times.

T HE ALARM WENT OFF at five. I found a newspaper outside my door and over a cup of Kona coffee and oatmeal cereal I scanned it for mention of the shooting. There was no mention. I showered, dressed, collected my gear and went downstairs intending to wait for Libby.

I needn't have bothered expecting any wait. She sat in a red convertible Chevrolet, her thick wooly hair tied behind her head, safari style. She got out and came to hug me. She wore a white button-down blouse with short sleeves, tan shorts and socks with boots and looked as I had seen her last - tough, unassailable and focussed. We hugged. She was tense steeling herself for something she or we would have to face. Straightaway I knew it was a bad case.

"How bad is it?" I asked, as we climbed into the bucket seats and started off.

"Awful." A cigarette burned in the ashtray. She picked it up and jamming it into her mouth, she cut across three lanes, narrowly missing drivers, and sped to the highway. "I spent most of the night looking at photographs. This is a boy. He's dead. He's a kid, a nice looking suburban youngster whose parents are probably frantic trying to decide where he is and why they haven't heard from him."

"How is he related to this teenager you were describing?"

"He was seen with him hours before the body was found."

I was quiet. I wasn't the type to go to pieces over a disgusting homicide scene and neither was she. We had tromped through grassy villages and slept beneath palm trees and listened to gunfire on and off throughout the nights we were there and then had encountered dead children slaughtered by gunfire. In the black and white photos Libby had taken the scrawny bodies and tumbled graves spoke as loudly as the look of fear stamped into their stoop of shoulder, body shielding body, hands covering the faces of children and infants. The war was a mess and I had learned much that spring about keeping my voice quiet about things I wasn't supposed to know, or see.

S HE THRUST THE PHOTOGRAPHS of the dead boy into my lap. The boy lay on top of the Great Wall as though someone had made an offering of him to the gods. He was ten or eleven, thin, undernourished with a cavernous ribcage showing through. The body was waxlike as though it had been drained of blood.

"Unbelievable, isn't it, that someone could do this to a child?" Libby said, as she sped toward the Honolulu airport. "It takes everything out of you to realize this is a young child. Not like the slashed bodies we saw all those years ago."

I didn't find it any less disturbing. "I have a hard time picturing someone carrying a body this far from the lot without being seen."

"I doubt the boy was carried. He was murdered there."

Long before I learned I was immune to the dead, I had been sent to San Francisco General to talk to hospice patients. HIV was breaking headlines then and I saw more than I wanted to for the age I was at the time, a somewhat naive twenty-two. "You think he was part of this pedophile ring the teenager allegedly belongs to."

"Yes. A sex slave most likely."

Over the years I would remember the startled expression on Libby's face as the Cobra lifted high above the trees and cruised at three hundred feet above the Tien Giang River and tiny villages. The man Mun had joined us the previous evening. In broken words he talked of soldiers sweeping down from misty snow capped mountains at the border of Cambodia in the night with torches and of the panic they invoked as the twigs beneath their feet broke their otherwise silent footfall. We stayed up the night at the Continental Hotel off Dong Khoi Street trying to decide whether to take a posse after them or to leave and by dawn we decided the best offensive was no offensive. As we gazed upon the forest we would live in for a month we saw, or thought we saw, an old man running beneath the trees. Libby had urged the pilot to descend to a hundred feet for a closer look. When the jeep pulled into the clearing and the standing man with a rifle pointed at us, I knew by her expression the village had fallen.

Libby came to an abrupt halt at the airport and we strode to an awaiting helicopter to fly to the Big Island. The pilot was experienced in the cockpit. He maneuvered a few glides and descents that left me shaken but as he honed in over the crime site I saw a small crowd had gathered nearby a mobile forensics van, along with a number of police holding back siteseerers on the beach.

A Lt. Kane Hanoka'a cleared us. He explained a morning rain had left the entire scene damp and to watch out for slippery stones and mud on the path. This said, he opened the gate and we passed through.

"He's the best officer here. He's in his late fifties, grew up here at Hilo and left to become a police officer in San Francisco until two years ago when his father died."

I took in the information. It was clear that as soon as he received the toxicology on the blood and urine, Libby intended to contact him for an inside look at what island police thought had motivated the killing.

"He allegedly has been tracking a series of kidnaps from Portland to San Diego," she added.

"What leads him to believe this is connected?"

"That's what I think. It's not public information yet."

"You've got some good informants."

"They're sources," she countered, to indicate she was talking to FBI or some other officiate.

As I followed Libby along the path that led to the towering replicas of the Refuge gods, I snapped photographs. From a distance I zoomed in on the courtyard of the reconstructed temple Hale-o-Keawe. At the end of the inlet the azure water was clear enough to see through to the sand and rocks. A large outrigger sat on a straw mat beneath an overhang also of straw. In the moment we passed beneath grimacing wooden replicas, their long stern faces huge distortions of ancient masks, Libby was lighting another cigarette, talking into a cassette recorder, waving to an officer who stood at the entrance to the small village.

She drew him aside as I stepped into a spot covered by bark on the ground and surrounded by palm trees. I climbed onto a wooden stage in order to better see the top of the Great Wall. There wasn't anything to see. The child's body had been airlifted to a morgue and a forensic technician from an Evidence Recovery Team had chalked in white powder lines where the boy's body had been laid to rest. At length Libby joined me. Cigarette dangling from her mouth, she climbed onto the stage and glanced behind her as though to measure the distance we had come.

"I see your point," she said, nodding to me.

"Even if the boy were killed here, lifting him onto the wall had to take Herculean strength."

"No, you're right. My guess is there was more than one killer. Two or three."

I gave a nod. "With all that effort, desecration was the point."

She nodded more to herself than to me as she lifted herself onto the wall and stretched out on it. The smoke from her cigarette spiralled into the air. From her height all one would have an impression of was the forbidding height. She climbed down with my assistance.

"C'mon, let's go," she said, and steered me by the arm to the stairs and then through the site to the path that led back to the lot. "They found the body yesterday. My source indicated the body was icy. You up for a trip to the morgue?"

A S I APPROACHED THE FREEZER, I could see the skin was actually translucent with numerous tiny blue veins showing through. It was simply the child's fairness, I thought. The shock was in viewing the bony face. The sculpture of the facial bones was unattractive, harshly french around the mouth and perhaps swiss or germanic around the forehead, eyes and cheekbones. It made for a swarthy look, an underfed appearance whether or not in reality the boy was under nourished in life.

He was tall for his age, perhaps five foot two or taller. His blond hair was silvery, straight, with a flaxen texture to it, cut above the ears and above the eyes. Brushed backward his forehead was broad and his temples protruded. He had been suffocated because there were no marks on him to indicate a stab wound or self-inflicted razor marks at the wrists or on his arms. His feet and legs were beginning to turn green.

Taking a deep drag on her cigarette, Libby counted the number of veins cracked due to injection. "Five places a boy of his age injected himself," and pointed them out to me. "And look," pointing to the sides of his feet which were a grayish color, and also interspersed by hairline veins.

The Medical Examiner was a small man in his seventies with a dark brown page boy cut and a dark moustache. He too believed the child was part of a group of abductees who had been sold into sexual slavery somewhere else in the country and brought to the islands either by the individual he was sold to or for such an exchange.

"You think something went wrong?" Libby inquired.

"No, in whatever ways he was used, he is now been discarded."

"Rather harsh discipline."

He shrugged, as if to remark, what was one to do? "There's an injunction on my cutting him open," he informed Libby, and then in response to her inquiring glance, he replied, "By the state. They want him on ice until the circumstances of his death are answered."

So they were unclear, perhaps not as to actual cause of death but to the level of involvement he may have had with a ring.

"I understood that a teen involved in a shooting was seen with him hours before he was discovered dead." Libby persisted.

"Not my department. You'll have to take up the matter with Honoka'a. He's in charge. He can tell you what tips have come in."

WE AREN'T GOING TO PRESS on this one until I can get an ID on the kid," she said, inside the helicopter. "I'm going to run an alert to every last elementary school in the country to see where this child may have gone to school and who the family is."

"Anything I can help with?" I shouted above the roar of the motor.

"Dig up every damn thing you can come across on Online juice bags." And then clarified, "Someone has a chat room for the sale of sexual favors."

"I'll be at my laptop for a year," I shouted. "Viacom's your best bet."

"It's an outmoded system. Check on CLETS for runaways. By now someone would've reported a missing child."

When her pilot landed and we disembarked, the air was heating up although the early afternoon had come and gone. We agreed time had gotten away from us. She dropped me off at my first interview at an apartment overlooking the waterfront about ten minutes outside of Pearl Harbor.

I checked my notes as I wound down the interview. Mara Tahiti had described for me at length the significance of burial in the Hawaiian world. When the first Kona king died, his bones were placed in the temple and he was declared a god.

Twenty-two other ruling Kona chiefs also had their bones interred there. Mara accommodated my interest, mentioning in passing that not far away, some three or four miles south of the refuge, stood the remains of a human sacrifice temple.

The basis for sovereignty, she said, was its system for conduct in the society. Accountability was to the ruler who segmented all parts of the land to various members of the royal community and thereafter to families who to one degree or another worked for the royalty. When a member committed a crime this was instanteously known. Lawbreakers were cast out of the society at large and brought in a state of near death to a sacred place such as to one of the heius or to the place the British would later bring lepers.

With the overthrow of the Queen, the last royal descendants kept as much of their former society as was believed innocuous. The schools taught children of no less than twenty-five percent Hawaiian ancestry their past, recounting battles and wars and the advent of colonialism and joining the United States as the fiftieth state. Although the majority of Hawaiians, she acknowledged, wanted statehood, she believed that the closeness of small communities of islanders was in fact kept intact by a rigorous training of the two languages and close tabulation of the state congress to assure all industry was profitable and not subject to competition. Thus, the orchid growers were few and far between, enabling them to gross millions a piece in trade; the fisheries that supplied the open markets and the gardens and cultural centers shared the economic stability afforded by growers of pineapples, macedonia nuts, and coffee along with windmills, beef and poi. She was pulling at the hem of her multi-colored quilt skirt to gather in the criticisms I might have as I sat down to represent her among the backdrop of current day culture. Even as I queried her about how Hawaiians of an older era struggled to contain their culture against threat of invasion I found myself seeking balance. If tourism accounted for the mainstay income, and food to a lesser degree, then as Hawaii left behind one form of government and put a gap of fifties of years between that form and the ballot box, they prospered as part of a society that was daily shaped by schools and school districts and by newspapers and communication networks and hydroelectricity and steamworks and NASA and satellite centers.

Mara was cautious to portray the ancients as ocean bound with rituals for building the boats necessary to hunt the fish. Fishing had marked the marketplace for hundreds, if not a thousand, years. As the modern world eclipsed the globe, it was natural that the social order her great grandparents and grandparents had come of age in was the one she would recollect in traditions including triathalon races.

I left knowing I had said too much and listened too little. I hungered for emotional distance between the boy's death and the article I had prepared myself for. The child took precedence, and the fact of him stole from my objectivity. I needed time and comfort between the two stories and something intangible to help me weather the shock I knew would arrive sometime during the night.

But the night was quiet. I fidgetted with my laptop and tried to enter a few chat rooms about voyeur sex unsuccessfully. Around ten someone knocked on my hotel door. I opened it to find no one there. When I returned to my computer I found a ghost had installed a web site without my permission and billed one of my credit cards for a hundred dollars. It was a Hermes Web deal. I decided when I entered I wanted a law enforcement cop at my side.

A YELLOW SEDAN PULLED up in front of the hotel. I recognized the passenger as Lt. Honoka'a. At his request that I join them, I got inside the backseat.

"Avia Hadom?"

"Yes," I replied.

"Detective Mike Lee."

I spied a copy of the Taiwan Gazette in Lee's jacket which draped the car seat. "You from Taiwan?"

"Honolulu. Born in 1946. Raised here."

"Alot of changes since then."

"More than you can imagine."

"Where're we off to?"

"Diamond Head," Lt. Honoka'a answered. "Libby will be meeting us there."

"Who else will be there?"

"Everyone on the forensic team including investigators."

Lee sped along the waterfront passing all the major hotels. We passed outdoor jewelry markets, painting galleries, shopping malls, apartments with gardens flowing from balconies, and board walks of harbor views. A ship sat at sea.

The place we arrived to resembled the state capitol on a smaller scale. It had a volcano shaped crown formed by twenty cantilevered concrete ribs with gold and deep red glass tiles.

The team the lieutenant had brought together were local experts. A woman named Chandra Green from the Medical Examiner office was there to report on forensic findings; there were fourteen officers assigned to the search for the boy seen accompanying the now dead child who had made contact with witnesses, and there were a psychologist, Laura Sojimoto, who was an expert on runaways and underground activity, a cybersex expert, Albert Zodril, on the technology, and two editors from The Sun Times, one of whom was Libby, the other was an undercover who handled crime assignments.

After the introductions, the lieutenant spoke about the various investigations in the western states which he felt might have a bearing on this death. The first, and most likely, were the kidnaps between Seattle and San Diego. These were of young children, most of them around age six at the time of the snatches, none were previously known to law enforcement nor to any therapeutic community. The FBI had been called in years ago when the second child was discovered to have matching profile to the first and they had focussed on mobile perpetrators.

A mobile perpetrator, the clinical therapist explained, was a special strain of psychopath who wandered from state to state and was a stalker, or what psychologists commonly referred to as an organized nonsocial perp, a deviant who could charm a child to leave their familiar neighborhood with a perfect stranger.

The forensic tech was a Hungarian woman in her forties. Tall, with brown curly hair and soft green eyes, she spoke with a faint clipped accent about taking several blood and tissue samples. Her findings revealed traces of cocaine and methamphetamine in the boy's bloodstream in sufficient doses to render him semi-conscious at the time of death. She also found the presence of ketamine.

"What's that?" The undercover detective posing as an editor asked. He was Pete Weekes and had blond curly hair and was five feet nine inches and had just turned fifty.

"Ketamine," Chandra said, "is a drug veternarians give to animals who are going to undergo minor surgery. It allows for anesthesia while permitting the animal to remain mostly conscious."

"Is it given to adults?"

"Never, and never to children. In a person it would freeze the muscles without denting their alert state."

"Deadly."

"Yes."

"Was it cause of death?"

She shook her head. "We don't know without an autopsy to look for the presence of trauma."

"But if it were the cause of death, it would mean this child was administered a final injection?"

"Yes."

Chandra continued. A full body of Xrays was taken. There were no fractures nor breaks. In life Chad had been healthy.

At the advice of the Medical Examiner, the dead child's photograph was matched to those who were kidnapped. He was not one of the snatches in that case. Nor was he allegedly kidnapped. She had wired every known jurisdiction in the three western coastal states and received a tentative identification. His name was Chad James, from Crescent City. The parents were flying in to view the body to make a tentative identification.

Libby had wired school districts and come up with similar information. Chad was the second son of a working class family that had relocated from Oakley to Crescent City in the last five years. Midway into the semester the child was allegedly placed in a more restrictive educational setting according to the mother.

Albert Zodril speculated it was possible that families facing financial difficulties were releasing children into the hands of these pedophiles or traders. He described the crime of engaging in illicit sexual activity on the Net as far more complex than most people understood it to be. He said most people involved in this crime were men living on the edge, that they were so obsessed with the Net they had no time to be with themselves or their families and that they had deprivation identities. By the time these men became unwitting victims of cyber technology they had overextended credit, were avoiding their mail, had difficulties with the IRS, had creditors lining up outside the door, were compulsive shoppers frequently buying things they didn't want or need over and over and some had joined Debtor's Anonymous to get a handle on their spending and fantasy life.

The victims were seldom the doers and the group knew on some level that even if Chad's parents had tried to hide the fact their child had been kidnapped, it was far fetched to imagine his mother could have handed her son over to one or more perpetrators.

KAI ROBE TALKED FOR over an hour. She was dead set against nuclear testing in the Pacific and had been trying for years to interest Hawaiians in adopting a French platform. The Hawaiians she believed had been hoodwinked by haole interests. These were the ruling class who favored annexation to the United States over remaining a royalty. Her friends had gone by boat to the atolls to demand a cease-fire and were rumored to have capsized at sea. France was the only government she knew of that did not test weapons. They paid Figi and the Cook Islands to remain nuclear free.

I WAS LATE INTO the night writing the positions for sovereignty. By midnight I sent my draft containing two thousand words by E-mail to the Concord desk. I knew before I received David's response there were large gaping holes unexplained by either woman's fervent desire to see an autonomous Hawaii. For one, the nuclear testing in the Marshalls, Belau, Enewotek and Bikini made life there virtually uninhabitable but the death sentence did not appear to greatly affect Hawaiian waters. If the wind currents carried ash certainly the hospitals would see more burn victims or higher incidences of cancer, which they did not. Cancer was actually low in the Hawaiian Islands, relegated mostly to those who worked with isotopes. For another, economic control and cultural identity and continuity, viewed as lost to America, would not be enriched without testing. Somewhere in this was a hidden reality that banked the future. It was clear to me by the time I went to bed I had not scratched far enough below the surface to understand what testing did in fact control.

I awoke to Libby's call. She was downstairs in the adjacent restaurant. I showered and dressed in a tan linen pant suit and went to join her.

She was seated inside a booth overlooking a pleasant garden. She had chopped off her hair. Oddly it looked better than when she wore it long. The frizzy texture was gone; in its place a temperate, somewhat coy appearance. She was dressed for a trek in brown pants, a windbreaker and army boots.

"You look great, sweetheart," I said, and slid in opposite her. "You get any sleep?"

"Six hours. What can you tell me about sovereignty?"

"Focus is too small. Other than that, they have some worthwhile ideas."

"Any direct knowledge of Figi and Cook Islands?"

"None, except they don't want testing there. It's giving everyone there cancer. If you'd like I'll line up an interview with the other side so you can understand where the two views meet."

"That'd be great." The waiter came and I ordered coffee. "What's on today's agenda?" She cut me a piece of her omelette and passed it to me on a bread plate.

"Chad was enrolled in a bungalow school for four months on the Big Island. I'm willing to cut you in for a piece of the action if you can accompany me."

"You realize of course I have about three more days."

She grunted an assent. "If this is going where I think it is, your boss'll give you another five."

"Can we discuss it here?"

"We've had a handful of deaths with no leads. There's

been a zone on printing any stories although we continue to receive leads. The paper brought in a handful of under cops to tip the police to investigations but so far nothing has been substantive."

The waiter brought my coffee. I added a touch of cream. The omelette aroused no hunger but I tore off a slice of garlic bread and washed it down with coffee as she continued.

"Originally the deaths were called in as elderly men found in flophouses. One day when the under was in the field I took a call at his desk and went through his files. I learned these were not men but in fact pre-teens. They were found in back rooms of salons and speakeasys and had almost no clothing on their persons. My belief is this kidnap stuff is an FBI cover to mask what's really going on."

"Very thorough."

She grinned. Lines around her eyes and mouth momentarily deepened. She was attractive despite all the time she had spent in death camps and hospitals. Her thin forehead, high cheekbones and thin jaw used to make me feel somewhat self-conscious because of the two of us she was prettier. But by the time I reached the age she had been when I first met her I had long possessed my own style and felt I could outstrip any face with my endurance and guts.

"So this child can be traced to a school. It suggests he found some stability among his captors."

"There's no telling. Did you give any thought to our briefing with the police?"

"I did. I decided because ketamine is an exotic drug there must be a veternarian in the picture."

"Or an asshole on the island who leaves the door to his medical office open."

"Could be that too."

"But you'll stick with the vet. Any idea as to why he'd stick his neck out so far?"

"None."

"Well," she said, spreading strawberry jam over a piece of garlic toast, "my guess is this is a fairly sophisticated group. Men who want children through this means are married and the wife acts as a cover for some reason. Could be they are criminals on the lam or worse, real pedophiles who ran away from their communities and are starting over here."

"Or who arranged the death of a spouse and left with the child or children who have since grown up and have had children themselves, perhaps by this same man."

"Jesus! Who in their right mind would go that far?"

"If you have to survive, sometimes the options aren't that numerous."

"Ready?"

I finished my coffee, grabbed a piece of toast, and we left.

By the time we arrived to the Big Island, it was ten o'clock in the morning. The sun was a pulsing orb and the temperature was pushing ninety. I had forgotten to bring a hat or lotion and purchased one at the airport tourist store along with a yellow and white gardenia lei for myself and for Libby. Libby purchased lunch.

We rented a jeep and I drove. We took the main road from the airport past burning sugarcane fields and a sugarcane plantation to a dirt road that took us far into the reaches of a forest which consisted of bony thin trees and dense grass. Here and there small thatch houses with yards appeared alongside the road. A herd of cattle crossed the road, and we had to stop. As we climbed a steep ascent and gained both distance and height above the island, the fields that stretched out below showed themselves not only to be a wilderness jungle but as we climbed higher around a bend, we saw crisscrossed fields, some dark green, some fertile brown the color of coffee. Libby thought aloud they were predominantly poi and crops and others were banana and mango trees.

The road leading to the schoolhouse was marked. I followed a bumpy course and parked at the end of the road where a red house was situated along with a long house made of brick blocks. We got out and looked around. The place had an abandoned feel to it as though a group of ten to twenty people had made camp for any number of months and then packed their belongings and moved on. Chances were they were not Hawaiians, nor islanders from a distant Tahiti.

After twenty minutes of eyeing the ten cots, the shower stall and wash basins, of examining the makeshift plumbing and severed lines to what was once a hot water heater fueled from the ground with logs, we decided could draw relevant conclusions about their situation. I took photographs of everything Libby felt was important including the writing on the chalkboard in the one room schoolhouse. Then I labeled my notebook with corresponding descriptions.

We scouted through the surrounding brush but finding the density too thick to penetrate we decided it was unlikely teens, children or adults had utilized the location in any other way. Overall it was a good hideout. The spot afforded the group some semblance of normalcy while retaining necessary vantage points for lookouts to see the road as well as to gaze upon fields and in one spot the distant ocean. Without interference life could be lived for a while.

"They didn't want to promote comfort," Libby said, as if reading my thoughts.

"I agree. Perhaps it was a control thing, they would lose their ability to sell the children."

"I'm going to speculate the children were grown. Chad may have been the youngest."

I considered this. "Could be they killed him because he ran away."

"There would've been signs of a struggle. I think he was a willing victim."

We divided the vanilla yogurt drink into equal portions in paper cups and each took a half cheese sandwich. I discovered I was hungrier than I had expected I would be and wolfed down my half and finished part of hers. The chocolate covered macroons tasted fresh and I reminded her my first meal when I returned to the states in 1970 was meatloaf, salad and macroons and coffee.

As we descended through the brush, Libby at the wheel, I glimpsed another road. We went down it more out of curiosity. It led through high grass to a shack wired with cables and detonators. A sign warning of trespass had been slapped over the front door which was nailed shut.

We returned to the road thinking the group could have left when the adults discovered the proximity of this shack to their establishment. I borrowed a cigarette from her purse and lit it and thought about the longterm problems of living on the run, because that is clearly what this group was doing. Despite the number of wilderness areas, at some point sooner rather than later it seemed, the group would be discovered. They would run out of places or they would be led to a camp from which the feds or local law enforcement could contain them.

I knew I wanted to ask her undercover associate out to pick his brain and knew in the same instance I wouldn't because I didn't want to run a risk of contaminating my relationship. Laughing I told her. She shrugged saying she had gone out with him once. He wasn't all that good in the sack.

I FOUND LT. HANOKA'A at the Honolulu precinct. He gave me a tour of the two story building and some tips on how to treat an article on sovereignty. The police were opposed to these people. They viewed them as interlopers who became involved as a result of opposition to slash and burn policies that resulted in the growth of sugarcane, the profits for which rarely came to the Hawaiian people. It was unfortunate that the sovereignty activists were neither the progeny of flower growers as he was, nor of fisheries or of landowners who raised poi or beef. They wanted more than one seat in the state assembly and would probably get it. After that, they did not represent enough business interests to influence many in the population at large.

Hawaii had not changed all that much in terms of population numbers in the last thirty years. The Chinese still carried the lead, followed by Hawaiian Polynesians and Hawaiian Americans. Trueblood Hawaiians were a race of the past with less than seven percent of the population.

"You married?" He asked.

"Divorced. Traveling alone," I added, when I saw I had somehow failed to answer his question.

"My mother owns an orchid plantation south of the Brigham Young Cultural Center. Perhaps you'd like to visit her."

"I would."

"Pack your things. I'll take you there first thing in the morning."

"It's a generous offer," I said.

He smiled a winsome smile that took years off his tired, harried appearance. "My mother will have fun with you."

"Does she have a phone at her house?" I asked, not knowing whether her home was located on the flower plantation itself or she had business agents selling her crop from other locations.

"Yes. She sells to the cultural center and to the Mainland. We've arrived to 2002 with everyone else."

two

"KANE, I'VE WORRIED FOR YOU!" Mrs. Honoka'a hugged her son to her.

She was a small woman with a large chest and thin calves dressed unexpectedly in tight black knit pants and a long flowery, blue and pink overblouse. I felt a little envious of their affection for Kane, which she pronounced Ka-nee, was clearly the favored son. Next to her he gained an air of ease causing him to seem thinner inside his tan uniform. She reached for my hand and took me into the house.

Framed photographs of the members of her family lined the inside wall. The first room on the right was a large living room with a fireplace and large tinted window looking onto a veranda with lounge chairs and past it at the front lawn and road where Kane had parked his patrol car. The rectangular lawns on either side of the walkway were headed by flowering shrubs and straw palms, their leafy shapes shadowing the bamboo-enclosed veranda up several stairs. The room on the left was a study with shutter doors half hiding a stereo and speakers and a computer on a cherrywood table that was situated beneath stained glass windows that faced the jagged mountains and slash ravines of Oahu. Mist had gathered on the mountain causing the green flanks to seem lush from ample rain.

We stepped into a large dining room and kitchen that, except for a small bedroom off the bathroom on one side and a pantry on the other, extended across the width of the small home. The floors were made of greenish tile and the walls of warm honey colored wood. Small lights emanated from the ceiling. The countertops were blue tile and she had two stainless steel sinks which were filled now with fruit and corn ears in preparation for the afternoon meal.

Behind a patio and manmade waterfall built into a concrete retaining wall with glass and tile lay the twelve acres of greenhouses inside which the family raised a million orchids a year. Several other houses the same size as Mrs. Honoka'a's sat at equal distances skirting the plantation. I remarked at the rows of greenhouses, and Kane told me approximately ten gardeners worked fulltime and another five at duties taken up by seeding and potting. The family gave tours one saturday each weekend which gave them cash for operating expenses. Because of their proximity to the Mormon cultural center they provided approximately three thousand orchids a year at the price of nine dollars and fifty cents a piece. Added to this, they shipped orchids in freezer units to five cities on the west coast and throughout the East coast including to New Foundland and Quebec. Only a percentage went to Japan and Hong Kong. Receipts minus cost of shipping was two dollars a flower.

Quenan Honoka'a had been raised by a preacher who tended orchids when he wasn't preparing a sermon or calling on the sick or needy. As the island became more populated the land his mother had secured working a land grant for a flower grower in Kauai became increasingly valuable until her son purchased his property outright. The soil was purchased from the Big Island as were the fertilizer and chemical additives. He had scripted his daughter Quenan into his business early when she was age ten and although she married twice and had two sons, she maintained a vigil from sunup to sundown attending to the day to day affairs of the plantation. Competition was a monster and every year the cultural center threatened to grow their own flowers in hopes of trimming their costs but the state kept a watchful eye to insure independents could compete.

Over lunch they talked about sacred heiaus, about gardens and fishing and about the Buddhist Church to which Kane's mother belonged and trips she made to Diamond Head and Honolulu to visit her grand children and great grandchildren. She no longer used to worry about overcrowding in the cities as she used to nor about the high cost of living and the scarcity of available jobs for the grand children who had left the orchid farm. She had stopped mailing checks after she saw one grandchild become severely addicted to heroin.

Kane left after the big meal. Quenan showed me the guest

room which had a small balcony and overlooked the sleeping giant that lay hidden in the mountains. She made tea for me and I sipped it in solitude as I sat on the balcony and looked at the greenhouses and the flanks of the mountains rising above the fields. Hers had to be a hard life with frequent worries, among them blight, freezer breakdowns on the cruise ships and airlines, and loss of trustworthy employment.

I slept for an hour. When I awakened I placed a person-to-person call to the Concord desk and receiving only the answering message line I put in a call to the senior city desk editor in San Francisco.

"Nice piece, Avia," he said, when he came on the line. "Dig a little deeper; see what their idea of the penal system is."

"Why?"

"You've touched on everything but."

"I doubt whether they have opinions," I said.

"I'm sure they must. Their sacred worship places are all about common people who are forbidden to utilize the roads that the kings used and temples where criminals were not allowed to set foot in or they would be put to death."

"History for the kings."

"Dig around anyways. Look for why they spend so much of their mythology on this subject."

"Okay," I said with a laugh. "Did you read my footnote on the child murder?"

"*That's* your story, Avi. Any idea why this fucker chose the Great Wall?"

"Sacrifice to the gods."

"That's why I think you should scrape the surface for the

penal system. City of Refuge was one spot where evildoers were condemned. They don't drown these men nowadays. Everything's above-board. That's why these trials are so goddamned tedious."

"Can you give me an assist? Any link between these computer sex slave groups and places of magical worship?"

"I have one person out sick, another on maternity leave."

"Thanks for the tip," I said, seeing a world open up. "Can you tell David I called?"

"Will do. Does he have your number?"

"I'm somewhere new," I said, and gave him the number.

I went to the library and put in an hour in the reference room. It was without a wall and faced an outdoor wilderness of slate, sculptures and flowering plants. Truly beautiful. I came up with a few leads on royal burial grounds and sacrificial rocks. Without thousands of families squeezed into small communities, the idea of royalty seemed to me an easier, more advantageous way to know who was doing what to whom. A criminal could more easily be accounted for. In addition the mines were controlled by the royal family as were the fisheries, canoe and outrigger enterprizes along with clothing and furniture crafts people. Very little was left to chance.

From my cell phone in my car I called Kai. She was the more challenging of the two experts on sovereignty. She said that although criminals were killed outright she was in favor of a more lenient, separate colony where criminals could live without having contact with the society they had left.

"How reasonable do you feel this would be?" I asked. "How

many car bombs, thefts, damaged property, attempted homicides, or arsons do you feel you could accommodate?"

She didn't have to think about it. She was a home owner. "None."

I contacted Mara who said sovereignty addressed the culture and the environment but not lawbreaking. It was a weakness in the philosophy. She couldn't offer a solution. She agreed with punishment but felt there were too many prisons. In her mind's eye the penal system would be less harsh, would offer programs for the children of the accused and would try to reform the criminal to live peaceably. It could work if no one had been murdered.

I called Libby after I returned to the Honoka'a estate and awakened her.

"We're growing up to be two lonesome old ladies," I said.

"Ha! One of us will win a Nobel."

"Not without a lead to try your unsolved cases."

She sobered when I told her where I was. "Get her to tell you about soldier camps. Ask her where they were and how you could gain access to them."

"Kane's probably already asked, wouldn't you think?"

"Avi, take nothing for granted. If he has, research it anyway. Especially for ways a group this size might move from island to island without attracting attention."

"What're you doing?"

"Running down this teen from hell. We've been in the chat rooms for hours today. Kane has officers on the street literally flagging down any and every teen that plays the videos at the arcades. Tomorrow they're up and running with fishing boats to and from the Big Island."

"They've probably made it off the island."

"You're getting negative, Avi. Call me."

I said I would. I was feeling negative. I put on a kimono and went to the kitchen where Quenan was darning a pair of knit socks. "What can you tell me about soldier forts?"

She gave me a queer expression before she answered. "They holed up inside the tunnels." When I didn't reply, she said, "The government put them in all over the islands. Today only two or three are open."

"Can you show me on a map?"

If an internal voice told her to stay away from the matter, she did not refuse. She went into her study and returned moments later with a tattered worn set of maps for the islands during 1938. She sprawled them on the table top. I eyed the rugged landscape taking note of the notations she had marked on the maps.

"May I review these?" I asked.

"We mined the waters," she said. "We destroyed the fish traps, held munitions in underground bunkers, set up telescopes in the mountains."

"Has your son told you about the case he is on?"

She shook her head, and bent it.

I took her denial as a yes. "The police have come across a number of teen murders in abandoned places and back rooms of bars and clubs that are unexplained. My friend and I have encountered a camp we feel these teens may have been taken to. It is empty today but there were sightings of at least one child while they resided there."

"The tunnels are buried," she said, when I was finished speaking. "You can't get to them."

"How many people do you suppose have knowledge of their whereabouts?"

"Anyone who grew up here during the war."

"Anyone else?"

"People like my family who had title to the land. There weren't many people living here then."

We were quiet while she continued thinking. Finally she said, "Doctors who served."

"What can you tell me about veternarians?"

"On the Big Island they were the same as regular doctors." She scratched her forehead. "They were the ones who brought in medical supplies to Oahu."

I took notes as she recalled the various Red Cross stations and the informal outposts which masqueraded as dance halls or boat repair shops. Everything that could be was placed inside a shack with a tin roof even if it sat in a channel or on the water. Once it was known Japan would be bombed for its role in the war, the Hawaiians upgraded these outposts placing them close to war-torn-looking buildings in and around Pearl. The tunnels, many of them set into the mountains, were meant to be utilized as lookouts as well as shelters if the island took additional artillery fire.

It was nine when Libby called. She was sending a limosene to pick me up. Another child had been found.

I GREW UP IN Berkeley, California at the start of the

out shelter at the Q Bar in a rundown basement of the Municipal Library listening to bombs landing somewhere north of where we were staying. In the morning the pavement had buckled beneath the bombing rendering steam rising from charred buildings. We had bundled up our belongings and fled south to another village.

"This one is a kidnap victim. The photo matches one we have on file."

"That proves it then. Who the child was travelling with."

"We can't be certain. It's possible the child was residing with a family."

Cautious to the last. All senior editors were. No one wanted information impeached by the public.

"He's thirteen. He's been missing for a good five years."

It didn't or couldn't register. Sometime after we went home though the shock would begin to sink in and I would feel the family's heartache and surmise the teen's terror. What sank in was the fact of where some of these children were. Kauai. Not Oahu. The kidnappers were still choosing remote terrain. Perhaps they knew nothing about tunnels used in the war or perhaps they did not believe the underground units held much protection for them.

We flew by chopper to Kauai to the mouth of the Wailua River. The death scene was a priest's house at a Tahitian temple where a partial restoration of reproductions of idols stood. Patrol vehicles, their blue and gold lights flashing on and off, stood in a parking lot. A group of officers huddled at the path that led to the site.

Bright lights in the lot and on the ground all the way to

the temple lit up the otherwise dark scene. A minivan was parked beneath a cluster of coconut trees and hidden from sight. The media had arrived but was being held back by a line of caution tape and several officers. Libby and I were one of the chosen who were allowed through. We followed the path a hundred yards to the sacrificial rock on top of which the body had been laid.

The boy's head had been shaved. One arm rested limply, hanging over the rock's edge while the body, too long for the stone rested awkwardly, the knees turned outward and bent like a macabre skeleton. It was impossible to distinguish the boy's features. He had been beaten badly. Bone showed through where portions of the skin had been bared. His checkered shirt and thin trousers were matted in blood to his torso.

An officer whose label read Maknamera came over to attend to my picture taking. "Gruesome death," he said.

Libby nodded, then turned back to her notepad where she drew a rough sketch of the victim. "Any possibility he got in the way of a boat motor?" She asked, as she shoved a cigarette into her mouth and lit it.

"Doubtful. He was probably beaten with a hard object."

"Okay. Any of you do a walk-through yet?"

"We were told it would be a waste of time. Too much bark, dirt and sand."

"I meant for a weapon."

"Not yet," he replied, and left to rejoin the group of detectives who were now walking up the path.

"Look at this," she said to me.

I came over to where she stood. I saw the deep downward

slash of a blade or something on the side of the boy's face. "Definitely a propeller. Small boat or outboard."

"Let's go before we get into an argument."

"Will Kane show?"

"My guess is they are going to conduct a superficial prelim, take flash shots and bring in a sketch artist and then bag the body. The feds won't arrive until tomorrow at the earliest."

I said, not to be impatient, "Let's wait. Let's see who shows."

"Okay, but it's going to be a long night. It'll be dawn before we take off."

Instinct told me to watch for chain of command. Normally the prelim detectives would show first, then the forensic techs, but these folks were coming from the different islands and some would not have use of a chopper before morning.

The lead investigator parceled out tasks after he surveyed the scene. He too thought a weapon might have been discarded nearby and ordered two detectives to give a grid workover. He ordered two rolls of film on the body alone, then shots of the interior of the temple with special scrutiny given to pieces of the temple or of the idols. After an hour the chief Medical Examiner arrived. He took blood samples and labeled them and then conducted a head to toe examination, palpating for possible fractures, studying the fingernails, lifting the clothing to view the body. Satisfied that pretty much everything that shouldn't be there wasn't, he ordered the body airlifted to the morgue in Honolulu.

He eyed Libby as he got up. "How'd you get the call?"

"It came to us."

"Really?"

I watched her eye his square set chin and wide angle of his eyes and his salt and pepper short cropped hair. He was African and Japanese.

"Really." She said. "The voice was of an adult male, probably Hawaiian."

"What'd you expect?"

"I'm seasoned enough never to expect anything. If the perp is Caucasian we go from there. If he is a Hawaiian of some type, we regard the picture from the angle that is suggested to us because of the evidence."

"Last time we talked —"

"I know," she responded, and raised her hands in protest. "But that was on an exotic cult thing."

"They're going to read this in as something similar when all is said and done," he warned her.

"I can handle it."

"Can she?" He asked, meaning me.

"Better than I. Nothing rocks her nerve."

He gave me a searing glance and I proved him wrong by glancing away.

"Do yourself a favor, Libby," he said, "and don't go looking for this sadist on your own. He won't be impressed by your need for detail."

As he walked off, I understood too late the reason Libby wanted to push off. "He's not the other guy."

"The Big Island has their own chief examiner. The other islands have to share him." She fumbled with another cigarette. "He's of the opinion women should not come out to scenes of child murders."

"He thinks men take it better?"

"They aren't the primary caretakers. When the primary caretaker in any family is a man he doesn't think they should be at the death scene either."

"Interesting notion. Is this why you wanted to take off?"

"He's going to invite me in for the cutting and he's going to expect me to watch from start to finish."

"He really wants to ram his ideas home, doesn't he?"

"I'm the only one who hasn't attended. He likes to know when he's awakened in the middle of the night that the entire crew is going to wind up with the same indigestion he is."

"I'd like to go."

"You won't say that after you see what happens to the body."

"What's he think about your under cop on staff?"

"He doesn't know he's there. No one knows."

"Why the secrecy from this ME?"

"You'd have to ask my city editor, Shelby Hong. She knows him and knows the situation."

I asked about the cult murder he had referred to. She said a young man, estimated to be in his twenties based upon the condition of his skin and thought to be a young baseball newscaster who had disappeared about six months earlier, was found dead at a cemetery on the Big Island, his eyes gouged out and his teeth removed. I winced, horrified.

"That was my reaction. I couldn't work a story for months. Dr. Harms advised me to get it out of my system."

"I get the idea. What did he say was cause of death?"

"Torture, because he could find no signs of strangulation or traumatic injury."

"Well, he didn't run away from his responsibilities."

"No, he didn't."

Her pilot took us back to Oahu. We took a cab to her condo. It was located on Ala Moana Boulevard in the top story of a Spanish style villa and overlooked the ocean from the living room and master bedroom windows. Hers was grand living on a grand style supported almost entirely by her paycheck. Because the mortgage took so much, she had little furniture. A white couch sat in the living room with a glass coffee table and a bed and computer in the bedroom. The guest room had a single wide bed and a chest of drawers with a clock on it.

Her husband joined us for dinner. He was low key, a man who had given himself over to the wheelchair which imprisoned him.

She cooked fried chicken with steamed vegetables and poi and we ate in the kitchen at a dark wood table with matching chairs in front of a fireplace that looked as though it could have replaced a wall heating unit in the hall had there ever been one. We were fresh out of words, although I knew the next pursuit would be to look for campsites where this group may have split into. It would have to wait. After the meal I went to sleep in the guest room listening to her wash dishes and stick them inside the washer and wipe down the formica counters.

I awoke in the middle of the night to find Libby sitting in the middle of her living room staring out at the darkness. I sat beside her and put my arm around her shoulder. In her silk pajammas she was thinner than I could have imagined, an angular frame that protruded at the shoulders and hips; tall, sleek and contained. I waited for her to speak. When after minutes she had not spoken and had scarcely breathed, I withdrew my arm and put a space between us.

"Dreams?" I asked.

"I haven't dreamed since Vietnam."

"You have flashbacks?"

"Something like that. The well's dried up." She sighed audibly. "I sometimes dream in black and white. The images tumble forward as still poses. I'm in trouble if I walk into a photo gallery of black and whites if the subject is a live crime scene."

An amputee. "Did you stay in touch with Nun?"

"For a while," she said, with a nod. "I went to his wedding when he was bethrothed to a Cambodian young woman and then to the dance celebration after. The wedding lasted four days and we slept on floorboards in part of her parents' home. It was a small three room apartment in the Mission."

I stared into darkness thinking about the winding river beyond the camp at Khum Angkor Ban in which the women cleansed their bodies and their clothes. The humility of a less wealthy lifestyle had made me humble in those days.

"Last I heard he landed a job with Bechtel as a programmer for their Vietnamese translations," she said. "I've been seeing a married man." The words shrank in the space between us. I'd have a hard time trying not to censure her, and she knew this. "I met him at a party at the open house for the new wing of the museum."

"You don't have to tell."

She laughed a hollow laugh. "I'd given up years ago trying to make it past him emotionally. He left his wife around the time these murders began and he's made an offer."

I was quiet, careful to maintain my own boundary. She'd come to a decision. It had compelled her out of bed into the living room. I knew her better than she thought and I knew she was allowing herself to move past him.

"My home is very sparse. I like living that way. For some reason he snagged me."

She wasn't the only woman I knew who became caught by the passions of the unattainable.

"I'd have to ask Sam to leave, and I've invested too much of myself to give up this place and him."

"Have you asked your editor for time off?"

"Not while this investigation is going on. Have you gained any insights into Kane?"

"No, why?"

She shrugged. "He married at a young age, or so I'm told, and she was caught in the tsunami that struck Hilo in 1960."

"He's older than I thought."

"He remarried but it didn't last."

We were silent. Moonlight spilled onto the water causing it to appear the color of a deep dark blue. I thought of returning to my room but did not want to appear rude.

"I peeked at your laptop," she said. "You have an E-mail waiting from one of those porn rooms."

I'd forgotten. "I was researching a lead you gave me on the first boy."

She crossed her legs and lit a cigarette. "Be careful. This

man arranges dates."

"With pre-teens?"

"I didn't ask. Do you own property?"

"A house. It's a quiet existence."

"What happened to your husband?"

We had been friends for years, before she relocated to Hawaii and dropped out of sight. "I left him. We disagreed on money and retirement."

"Any plans to remarry?"

I shook my head. "You?"

"If he's unattached and without difficulties." Then: "It's premature, Avi. I'd like to run off with the first single man I meet."

"You've never been impulsive before."

"It claws at me. He was more attentive while he was married."

Rebound stuff. It consumed me for the first three years I was divorced. "Any plans to retire?"

"You?"

"I'd like to write a book as my big bang," I said. "Then again, there's time. I have eleven years to go before my parole is up."

"Know just how you feel. I'm sixty-four. My time was up a year and a half ago. I just can't think to retirement. If I can target an assailant, I'll have a chance of going for a promotion."

"Get out while you have a life."

"Who has a life?"

We made our way to the kitchen. She opened a bottle of

Dom Perignon and poured two glasses.

"I've lost a handful of friends in the past five years," she lamented.

"I'm sorry."

"The world seemed alot more promising twenty years ago."

"Well, we get it figured out up to marriage and then if the marriage breaks up, there's no direction after. You're on your own."

She held her glass in a cheer. "They don't want to tell you how bad it can really get. You're supposed to have the smarts to find a man who is incapable of a life of his own."

"Always the pessimist."

"At least I'm honest."

The clock read twenty after midnight. It was Thursday. I had a day left, two or three if I was lucky and David my editor extended me the extra time.

Libby stared at the fluid in the bottle of her thick glass. "The condition of this child was very disturbing."

"Yes, it was. I haven't let it sink in yet."

"I've found the assignments have lives of their own. It will surface when your mind clears a space."

"You going in to observe the autopsy?"

"I won't be up for it. If you're smart you won't go in either. Watching the guts go into one bowl, the rip from the collar to the hairline, and the facial skin peeling off like a mask will leave you hollow for years, not just months."

"I thought you didn't observe a cutting."

"We saw a film of the procedure."

"That should've qualified. Did you tell Dr. Harms this?"

She shook her head. I realized after a few moments he was the source of her agitation.

"Is your friend Dr. Harms?"

"Oh good Lord no."

"Does he know him?"

"It's a small community for physicians."

If she had lied about where she met him, she had her reasons for doing so. I didn't want to learn them. I felt sorry for Sam. "I could've done without the gory detail," I said after a moment.

"I wish you'd let things alone. Stop dragging them around."

"Like the cutting?"

"Yes. And the prying."

"I didn't mean to pry. I can see you're upset. Shall I leave you alone?"

But it wasn't that. She was regreting having asked me to stay over. She could have put me in a cab and I would've returned to the Honoka'a farm. I knew her mood; I had put myself in the very same situation many times immediately following my divorce.

"No, it's fine," she said in a tone that begrudged any further communication.

"I'm exhausted," I said. "I'll see you in the morning."

"Good night, then."

I closed the door on her despair. If I awakened before she did I would hail a cab and see my way to the police precinct.

three

S HE WAS GONE when I awakened. I called my home
office and learned David was in the field covering an arson. It was that time of year when errant teenagers or the
criminal element burned half the unincorporated areas.

I left her a note and a twenty dollar bill to cover my phone
tab and food I ate. I hailed a cab on the corner and asked to
be transported to the Honoka'a farm where I picked up an
overnight bag, then taken to the precinct station.

I walked in as Lt. Honoka'a was walking out. "I want to
assist. I'm open to anything."

His hand caught me around the waist. "Your timing is
great," he said, and told me as we strode to his patrol vehicle
that the teen seen in the stabbing earlier in the week had
been seen on the northern side of Kauai.

There was alot of action breaking, he said as he checked

out at the checkpoint. Another teen, who looked similar to this young man, had returned to the scene of one of the first unexplained teen deaths asking about him. The club owner put his own employee as a tag on the teen and supplied him with a walkie talkie. And finally a kidnapped child had been identified at a country store on Kauai.

"He came in here real intrusive like," said the club owner, a man named Chilton who looked as if he had crawled out from under the pavement of the Haight-Ashbury in San Francisco. "Sit me down with a sketch artist and I'll give them a description."

"Let's start with the teen himself."

"He's an Asian wacko, well known around these parts for S&M encounters. Apparently you buy him off the Internet and he arrives with a carrying case of chains, whips and drugs. He tied this guy up in his motel room, beat him, fist fucked him pretty badly, nearly killed the man, then stuffed a sock in the guy's mouth so he couldn't call for help. Guy wasn't found for thirty-six hours, when the maid came in to clean."

"Where can I find the victim to talk to him?" Kane asked.

"He's a businessman living in Hilo. He used to come down twice a year to talk to an associate. I didn't inquire more than that. A customer's business is his, until he parks his problems right under my nose."

"Got an address for him in Hilo?"

"It's an LKA. Last known address. He hasn't been back since the incident he was roughed up."

"What about the teen who died?"

"This teen wanted to check on him. I told the cops when

I found the body. It didn't make sense to me then. Doesn't make sense now. Why the hell'd they pick on my motel? Don't I charge enough to keep the riff raff at a distance? Sixty-eight a night isn't cheap."

Okay," Kane said. "We'll put you in Number 7. Whenever this teen leaves you follow. I'll have an undercover stationed in Number 1 and across the road. They won't take their eyes off you for a second."

I was ready. By noon the operation was ready to roll.

As soon as the activity dropped to a lull the teen made a dash for the street. I carried a book and moved as innocuously as possible, reasserting myself when he stopped into a bungalow into a purchased flamboyance with a rainbow colored hat and scarf and string of shells. He re-emerged on the street just as I finished paying.

He was with a boy, a preteen who was perhaps eleven or twelve, or older. The boy had a few pounds on him around the middle and thighs sizing him out. But he was handsome, a blonde with curly hair and an innocent face. The baby blue colors of his shirt and jeans intensified the sense of innocence.

They strolled down the block, two teens seeking their fortune. The Asian pointed out a handful of sights and the other one laughed. They stopped to purchase ice creams, then headed to the sea wall to watch the fisherman with their nets. From the corner of my eye I watched. They could've passed for gay; perhaps the intent was to eventually turn the blonde over to someone.

The undercovers moved into view. They were at once invisible and public. One approached me to ask the time. I got nervous and cut him off.

The Asian turned. His profile suggested he was New Zealander or islander, he himself deposited here by low functioning parents or separated at sea from his family. Whatever his life consisted of, it had given him excellent training for this moment. He nudged his friend who turned also and together they viewed the distant mountains rising high above lush green switchback trails.

I followed them at a distance into the evening. Instinct made me plant myself outside the Caucasian teen's room. I wasn't certain whether the Asian would be returning. I feasted on Blue Moon tropical drinks and salty pork and rice and thought about Libby's marriage, in tatters around her knees, kept in sick bay by an affair with a man I was certain she worked for.

When the jeep arrived another man whom I thought I recognized from somewhere went to fetch the teen, I was glad I'd trusted my instincts. Although I could not see them I knew the undercovers were nearby, shadows waiting a sign from a lead operative.

I grabbed my hat and scarf, set two twenties on the table and made a beeline for the car Lt. Honoka'a's team had supplied me with. In the darkness we made a line of red coals, striking into the darkness at intermittent intervals. There were no signs by which to know the journey. The beaches swept past, so did a plantation hotel, boats tied to a pier at Hanalei and a snorkeling outfit. At length the road darted inland over a short bridge and veered into a field of corn. The sickly smell of sugar aroused my hunger, then the senses died down and were replaced by a swift kind of terror at the quick realization I was headed into a trap.

I turned off the road and killed my lights. As a number of cars swept past, not all at once or together, I wondered whether it would do any good to stay the night. I decided to return. If I called Kane I'd have to do so long before I returned to the motel.

In the end I stuck to the original instructions. No phone calls, no notes. Routine surveillance. I let myself into my room. Through the thin wall I could hear the Asian in the shower, luxuriating in a long respite. Some ten minutes later he shut off the tap. A minute later the television came on, sound blaring. Instinctively I cracked open the door. Chances were if he had to leave he'd let the set volume on high.

Libby called once on the cell phone. By the time I answered it she'd rung off. I didn't return the call.

I awakened to the sound of a loud knock on my door. I jerked to an upward position as Officer Lee took the liberty of entering.

"Decapitation some fifty miles on the ocean side," he announced and perched on the edge of a rattan chair as I splashed cold water over my face.

"Have you informed Libby?"

"Everyone's flying in. The feds landed yesterday. We've had no time to debrief. We may as well have brought over platoons for the readiness we need to have."

I agreed. I donned fresh clothes - jeans, a lightweight top and a jacket. "Any idea as to time this may have occurred?"

"At least a week or two ago. There's wasp nests, second generation insect activity, a real mess."

"Jesus, who the hell is this animal?"

The road was wet from a predawn drizzle. Officer Lee took the same road I had followed the previous night. When we passed the Hilton plantation, its three story verandas and large windows, I discovered the dread in my stomach had become a tight fisted knot. I no longer wondered at the savagery this group of teens was capable of, nor at their intentions. They were surviving under someone else's tutelage. I knew damn well the physician investigating the case had propositioned Libby in order to stay abreast of current developments. If the FBI had flown in a command central, then it had staffed the case from the day of the cult murder the way it usually staffed exotic, potentially high profile homicides, with the appearance of too few agents to adequately handle the job. The agents were in place, probably as frustrated as an investigator had a right to be.

Lee turned inland crossing over the bridge. High on the hill sat a metallic gold shrine. We passed taro fields, the taro several inches deep in a pond. The ponds extended for miles putting a cleavage through rugged ravines dotted with sugarcane. I shot a round of photographs as we ascended, my head and arms out the window. The paradise, such as it was, provided an excellent cover for any filth that crawled through it or hid somewhere in the intersections where houses had been erected.

The road ended before a hillscape of dense foliage. With a grimace Lee indicated they had to descend some fifty to a hundred feet to the road that led to the house where the human head had been found because the road leading to that particular house was closed due to a mudslide.

I adjusted my backpack and started down the backside of the mountain behind Lee. The air smelled overpoweringly sweet and the dirt was covered with overripe skins of guavas, their fruit spilled out. A secure foothold was difficult due to the erosive quality of the ground and I slipped into Lee a few times. He tore off a branch and fashioned it down to a walking stick and used it to anchor his footfall. I imitated him tearing off a branch where I could find one, and we descended like dwarves, single file to the road.

It was true the road's access had been dented by mudslide but this also included a tree with its roots upended. The walk to the man's house was lush with moss and foliage that hid from view all signs of habitation. I told Lee about my pursuit the night before and he nodded saying he had heard about it from a senior officer for the Kauai State Police who had gone in up to the sugarcane field and then turned back, afraid to follow further. My nerves settled a bit when I heard this.

A crew of island police met us at the property. The house was built in an oriental fashion with a large black and gold door and brass dark red handles. Floor mats made a runway down the central hallway which opened unexpectedly to a large living room overlooking a garden and the ocean. The carpets were silvery tan and the furniture, also oriental, was sparse consisting of a golden and dark green sofa, a matching ottoman, and a glass table on top of which was an elegant green serpent and a glass see-through orb. Lt. Honka'a was there with Dr. Sojimoto from the forensic team speaking in low whispers to the owner of the house and property. He was a tall Spanish man with reddish skin and dark wavy hair which extended into a pony tail from his rather sharply angular face. He nodded to me as I stood at the top stair, my sense of propriety causing me to stand aloof rather than to charge forward. Officer Lee took me out the side entrance to the backyard where the head had been discovered by the owner.

The garden had once been walled in in three tiers. Today the concrete looked old and the grass contained inside each periphery was crab grass studded with purple wild flowers. At the cliff overlooking a black sand beach was a stone bench. The chalk lines showed where the head had been placed. Blue and red feathers still littered the path and were stuck to the stone by various colors of candle wax. I collected another roll on film before we made our way across the lawn to the edge of the garden.

From all sides the home accessed the black beach and aquamarine water. It was curious why this site was chosen. Lee speculated that it was Mr. Spinoza's business as a deep sea diver searching for lost expeditions off the atolls. Perhaps these opportunists understood him to have a basement display of antiques collected from Figi or Bikini, or perhaps despite logic they sought conquest of a powerful man as a method to bring the world of art and culture to its knees.

We walked slowly to the house. From the footpath the structure was reminiscent of a lighthouse, the large living room having been remade into a liveable square, the upstairs hallway like a strand of thick glass from which light emanated and then a series of gables of two or three bedrooms. It was a modest home, although decorative and spacious.

Johnathan Spinoza greeted me at the walkway. "Kane tells me he brought you to meet his mother."

"Yes," I replied. "I came to write an article on sovereignty."

"Ah," he said, his manner also tentative and careful. "First you must understand there are two laws, that of sovereignty and that of the courts."

"I was told the law of sovereignty weakly defines law-breaking."

"Well, that's the secret. A hundred years ago before Sanford Dole overthrew the queen to become first territorial governor, lawbreakers were expelled. Some were hurled off mountains. The Hawaiians permitted the British to send its lepers to Molakai. Remnants remain as to social treatment of criminals."

"You don't sound as though you agree."

"No one does. They are quacks."

"But they raise concerns about the degree of intermarriage."

"Don't let it fool you. The ancient Hawaiians are the most intermarried because they were a small society. They married Chinese, Japanese, New Zealanders, Australians, and recently Americans and Europeans. They were originally Polynesians." He laughed. "I overheard you two talking. I suspect it is the tunnels beneath the cliffline and the wilderness interior that gave some madman the idea to silence the few of us who have homes here."

"Do the tunnels lead to the interior?"

"They used to at one time. Today the best way to reach it

though is to take a horse trail in on foot. Is the name Hadom Israeli?"

"Originally. I'm American born."

"Well, if you're up to it you can join us. We've been discussing a search into the interior."

"Yes. I'd like to join you. Has the head been taken to a morgue?"

"No, it's in my cellar icebox until a medical helicopter can fly in for it."

I descended another flight of stairs to the underbelly of the house. An officer showed her the specimen. Packed in ice, the head resembled a large rutabaga, its blond hair matted to the skin. Feathers protruded from the eye sockets and open mouth and only bone and some cartilage where the nose and ears had been revealed the head was human.

I grabbed my throat in horror. "Oh Jesus! Who the hell is capable of such a thing?"

"It was brought to this sight," the officer said.

"Yes," I said. "It certainly was. How do you think the head was severed?"

He was detached. "Chain saw probably."

There were terrors and terror. I hoped it was not one of these children. I hoped also that the two teens I had seen the previous evening were incapable of such violence and evil.

I SLEPT IN awakening only once to the volleying sound of a car backfiring. The day was still young and the police having cited and detained the Asian from Number 6 were now all over the motel, clamoring in and out of rooms, having set up fax machines and telephones to handle the influx of information about the teen and suspected alliances. Libby had arrived with Kane, and they sat in a room across the hall discussing strategy and wolfing down chips and iced tea. I gave Kane a blow by blow, focussing on the direction the teen had been taken and conjecturing that in all probability he was to rejoin a group or to be turned over to an adult. Libby said she'd come across a known child porn camp somewhere south of Hanalei. Kane said we had an hour before rendevouz with the other detachment. We'd be going in three hours before sundown.

I took my time dressing. I put on a pant and long sleeved turtleneck top made of a light green windbreaker material. I tied my hair back from my head and painted my face with a pastel green face paint meant to obscure me from the leaves and grass. My sock cap was made of light green hose. I strung rope, nylon cinches, pencil light, a knife, and film to a waistband and tested it for snugness. I strung my camera over my back. Into my green backpack I crammed an inflatable bedroll, shamoi cloth and dried food in thin cannisters designed for survival in the wilderness. I included an empty cannister for refuse and used toilet paper.

We drove out in groups of five. We ditched our cars at the base of a well travelled road that led to interior waterfalls some five miles north and to the Kaanapali at the farthest reaches.

The trail meandered below an overhang of creeping vines and flowering ginger. The four men at the lead and two at the rear made a rope trail by hammering posts into the ground and attaching ropes through pegs that were attached to the top part of the posts. As we walked in twos the air grew cooler and thinner. We followed the officers in front of us, walking more deliberately attending to the gradations in color of the surrounding plants, noting the way the sunlight filtered in dappled and muted variances of light through the leaves. Emerald water dripped from crevices in the protruding rock and ran like a snake's skin over soil.

We walked for hours at intervals eating nuts and water and dried salami slices with dried fruit. When we came to a waterfall, we set our backpacks on the ground and took a breather. I counted twenty in our group. We were for the most part in our forties, born and raised somewhere in Hawaii or California, with high school and college diplomas, in addition to Administration of Justice courses for those who were neither law enforcement nor Federal Bureau. Most of us were currently netting forty to fifty grand a year, had owned homes upward of ten years and had put at least one child through college. This sameness I suspected gave us a similar outlook, holding us to similar tensions and a pervasive feeling that we were an instantaneous community.

WHERE THE POSSIBILITY of landslide was greatest we ran along the trail, pacing ourselves for uphill climbs and blowing out audible sounds as we pulled ourselves by rope to the first summit. If any children were camped out at this high altitude they had to be persevering athletes, mentally and emotionally cloyed to their abductor.

Night fell as a dramatic plunge. In sharp retort we snapped on headbands with strong light appliances. Once we adjusted to the dark we proceeded cautiously. When we found the camp our plan was to radio in for helicopter assist and then to descend like a band of screaming banshees.

We must have come fortuitously close to camp because as we discovered the grassy knoll we also heard snoring. We set our gear down camping in the raw as it were, fearful if we so much as said a word or unzipped or snapped open a sleeping bag we would be discovered.

The grey of dawn filtered down as a mist. We slipped on our backpacks and stepped through the grass filing into a lineup that could overwhelm a small band of teens if needed.

As the day encroached and the first light spilled from the East and poured into the canyons, we saw the beds of the camp. Whoever had been snoring had fled and it was doubtful they had been there at all because there was nowhere to flee to. There were however a good fifteen three by seven foot beds or graves cut from the soil with shovels. They looked like small trenches, or if seen from afar like giant imprints.

As soon as one officer scouted the entire camp and gave the whistle that no one remained, Libby and I sprang forward shooting pictures of the graves. We shot closeups, moderate shots and distant ones, used measuring tape to delineate height on film and lay inside the graves to shoot photos of the interior of these beds as one who was sleeping inside it might see.

Officers mixed and poured plaster of Paris casts; combed the area for signs of clothing, utensils, dolls or other indicators of who may have been here; and marked the area off with tape. Kane called the air base for a helicopter to retrieve the forensic evidence and was told it would be a good twenty minutes. As lead detective, Kane assigned tasks to break down the scene in to manageable assignments to assure nothing was overlooked. Officers slipped into roles as forensic technicians and with cassette recorders described what they saw. By seven o'clock the group had discerned there was no evidence of blood nor skin and that if a group of children and preteens had lived here for any length of time over two days there should be human wastes in detectable amounts for the serology people to type DNA and begin classifying teens by blood type.

W HAT WOULD A CHILD feel? Libby and I sat at an outdoor cafe on The Big Island where we had regrouped and sipped lattes and nibbled at scones. We had dismissed diets, good health and long life. Death's grip had set in and everyone who had gone up the mountain was beginning to feel the strain.

We conjectured disassociation would become all engaging as the child, upon realizing there was no escape nor return to normalcy, surrendered to the distortions the leaders of the gang wanted to perpetrate. A sort of amnesia would ooze out of the child like a feverish sickness. It would take hold becoming an essential survival mechanism after the first two or three years. Only fury would cancel the amnesiac weight. But once the young teens understood they too could be murdered their own fury would seem too strong, too consuming, and they would become afraid of it.

If they sought refuge in animals as a way to safely block

off the distortions, they might view themselves as birds, capable of fleeing, huge wings casting a giant shadow over the landscape, the ravines, cliffs and momentous ocean. Perhaps their fantasies would take them to peaks above the valleys, into the clouds or to some place where no one could rise high enough to, and they would keep their faces to the wind, would detach from the knowledge of their bodies, would permit being caught if that was the only way to keep going.

We talked late into the day and night, searching for words to convey the horrific. We laughed and smoked cigarettes and Libby cried about her marriage and her husband's paralysis. While she called Sam to say she loved him, I went out to talk to Kane and found him with a handful of Army men studying aerial reconnaissance film, all of them trying to identify who, what, when and where the people were and the safety of sending in teams to surround them. There were too many in the camps, more than six at each of two sights. Plus they were staffed with their own aerial abilities, possessed troposcatter artillery and positioning aparatus and had communications to a home base on both The Big Island and on Oahu.

Their side was winning and our side had lost yet another round. I thought I could go out and get drunk, and did. Halfway to a miserable headache a cute guy who I had helped lift plaster from several of the graves joined me. He said he was single and unattached and I believed him. We chatted about the normal mental development of children between the ages of nine and thirteen. He seemed quite an authority. I left a note for Libby and then went to his motel room and spent the night with him.

ANY POSSIBILITY THIS actually could be a cult?" Lt. Honoka'a asked the team.

We had regrouped in Kona at the Kamehameha Hotel at 0900 hours. Caffinated and decaffinated coffee and bagels with Canadian lox and creamcheese were served with pieces of melon, bananas and pineapple.

The psychologist was Laura Sojimoto. She was Japanese and had grown up while Hawaii was a territory. When it became a state in 1959 she was diagnosing school age children for problems in thinking.

"I don't think so," she said. "Despite the presence of cult objects and the finding of ketamine in one child —"

"Two," a detective who worked closely with forensics countered. "And evidence of Kau sand contained in the plaster."

"Despite this, these children have no marks to indicate they practised satanism."

"I think the site strongly suggests it," another female said.

"What we came across yesterday is proof of intimidation. These children have been sold by a porn group to businessmen who go in for a certain type of thrill. The men already have something wrong with the way they function. They either can't perform normally or they enjoy watching deviant behavior. The deviance the children were subjected to was meant to mask something else."

I asked, "Have the leads here and Oahu given you any ideas as to how the adults or ringleaders function?"

Kane answered. "We know they take victims directly off chat rooms. They try to bleed adults with young children dry such that sale of a child becomes a necessity. The rings we've tracked are dominated by Asian teens. What this is about we aren't really certain. The individual here is believed to run a card game. It's in a suspected meth house which means getting in and out is next to impossible.

"The plan is to conduct surveillance. If he is who we think he is we want him to try for at least one run. That way we can nail him making a transaction."

There was a silence. Then a flurry of questions.

Kane held up his hands. "One question at a time. Please."

"Does the group use geisha girls?"

"Do the Asian boys prostitute themselves or younger children?"

"Is there a preferred age?"

"When do the ringleaders decide a teen needs to come out?"

He addressed the last question first. "We think they opt out any child before majority age for obvious reasons. We also suspect they encourage fatherhood, possibly between a preteen and a fifteen or sixteen year old."

The next query came on the heels of his answer. "What about the johns? How does the ring handle them if they become attached and want the teen to live permanently with them?"

"The deaths occurred for reasons germaine to their operations. Since they have struck at two sacred places and at the home of a man who dives for precious art, we're treating their focus as exotic."

"But not cult."

"Correct."

"Any of this tied to imports?"

"We are checking into that. The drugs we think are manufactured on the islands. The problem in the past was the minute we came close to an operation of this size the diversion backed us into a corner with computer viruses, teen look alikes, voodoo, bookstore burglaries, you name it. Plus there were no deaths that we could link."

I drove at breakneck speed toward the easterly side of the island. The trade winds had died down taking with them an ionic charge that for hours, in addition to being cooped up, caused me to feel restless. The night had been respite for me, but seeing the officer during the briefing had reiterated that old addage I'd arrived to my middle years with. Leave the work crew alone.

I veered up an incline onto a road that led to a volcanic wilderness. Large volcanic rocks and stunted ohia trees whipped by, interspersed by frozen rivers of lava and large uninterrupted segments of the dark Kau desert. Time stretched before me. In the stark sunlight pieces of strewn timber looked like bleached bone.

I pulled over and got out. A wind had started up, carrying with it a noxious smell of sulphur. I crossed the road onto wind-rippled dark sand. Walking was slow and fatiguing but I bent, my head to the wind, and continued walking. This was Kau sand. How had this sand arrived inside those hollowed out beds or graves several islands away? And why would anyone bother? I bent to sift sand through my fingers. The heat warmed my back. Was a child killed here and no one had discovered it yet? I stared at the endless stretch of rippled desert. Drifts of sand swirled over the pocket where my hands had been, cancelling the pocket.

Overhead a helicopter traversed the area, no doubt with an aerial recon monitor in an attempt to discern graves.

I WAS ON THE PHONE to my editor for an hour. He advised me to forget about drug dens and computer porn. The public had been fed a steady stream of this diet for the past twenty years. It was old hat and no one cared any longer. He suggested I stick to the killings, tie them into something unique. I agreed and told him I was faxing sixty frames of film from the forensics laboratory.

"One more thing, Avi," David said.

"Yes?"

"Interview this guy. Kane. Talk to him about his personal life. When they apprehend the killers, it'd be nice to have him blocked out."

I found Kane running on the main road. He was my height but had a paunch and heavy legs. I fell into step with him. After a few minutes I decided he was in better shape, and I fell behind.

"My editor's not interested in the computer angle," I told him to which he chuckled and replied, "I don't decide the recipe for each case. It just happens to be here."

"Your mother worries about you."

"Well, I maintain a careful line between the work and my life."

"Is that from longtime experience?"

"I lost my first wife to a tsunami," he said.

"I'm sorry. Were you young?"

"Twenty. I had just joined the Army and we were stationed in Hilo. Word of it came over the radio. I told her to stay on high ground but she wanted to go down to the shore and watch it come in."

I waited hoping he would explain.

"It didn't come in at a foot as reported. It thundered in as a wall of darkness at a hundred miles an hour. It picked up cars and drove them into second story factory windows; it smashed the waterfront; it sliced houses in half. Seeing it from our complex on the hill, I thought I would be obliterated."

"Was her body recovered?"

He gave a nod. "She was the daughter of Hilo's sugarcane plantation. Her grandparents who had a veranda home on the waterfront were also killed."

I could not speak. When the story touched me personally I too became silent, removed and slow to respond.

"We had been married under a year when it occurred. I left for the Mainland as soon as I put in for a transfer and after a year at the Precidio, I entered a police academy. It's a long time ago."

"It is. I'd like to get a story from you that's publishable."

"Well, after the police academy I did a stint in Oakland for three years, then was accepted in Sacramento for eight years and finally went to work as an undercover for the feds in their San Francisco Division helping them track primarily rapists and arsonists."

"Why didn't you join the FBI?"

"I gave it a good deal of thought. I wasn't offered investigative work. They wanted to install me as a supervisor over-seeing a line of detectives."

"Why didn't you ask them for detective work?"

"I was well known to the divisions. They felt my familiar-ity with who was undercover could hamper my safety. You can't print that."

"In other words they wanted you for Internal Affairs?"

He gave a nod. "I felt it would be safer for me if I stayed in view."

We had reached the hotel. "Any marriages?" I asked.

"One. She was my secretary when I worked out of San Francisco. I took her with me."

It made me wonder. I thanked him and walked with him to the elevator.

"Off the record," he said, as we entered the glass lined elevator, "when we returned after my father's death I ran into one of the detectives I had worked with for a handful of years. He was out of Bureau work but had opened a private firm in Oahu and was making out quite well. He said he'd been of-fered the same deal and he'd taken it. It had apparently landed him here in the islands."

"I guess he wasn't cut out for supervisory work either."

We came to my floor and he stepped into the hall with me. "The point is San Francisco runs the Hawaii Division in most respects. At some point they will need to be consulted."

"That won't be a problem, will it?" Already I was think-ing ahead to an interview with my contacts at the division.

"Only if the business this ring is into conflicts with their recent closures in Hong Kong."

"1997 is a distant memory."

"Until the banks that gave the city its cash flow are sub-stituted elsewhere, the memory is never distant."

I looked inquiringly at him. "You think sovereignty was a plug for those banks taking root on the islands?"

"No. The economic community finds the sovereignty is-sue distasteful."

He was being polite and I was out of my depth. I thanked him again and told him I would rejoin the investigative team as it became useful. I suspected my usefulness however was close at an end.

He left me to take the elevator to his room on the floor above mine. I opened the door to the room I shared with Libby and found her asleep on a chaise lounge on the bal-cony. I showered and changed into pants and a blouse and then took the telephone and went into the hall where I paged David at his home.

"Whatever you can find," I said, about Lt. Honoka'a's problem in San Francisco. "I don't want to step on toes or wind up in a body bag."

"It's nothing, Avi. There was a big bruhaha six years ago over proper credentials. They suped everyone and went from there, but I'll check it and call you back."

Libby had awakened. She fished a cigarette out of her pants and lit it. Chewing on the end she said she thought I was a fool for having sneaked off with a detective.

"Not a detective. Local cop. No status," and jumped on the phone the moment it rang.

"Avi?" It was David.

I carried the phone into the bathroom this time and turned on the overhead fan. "What?"

"They had a leak on a major investigation which they thought they could stem by bringing in cops as unders. It didn't work, so they split the division into a few sidelines to track the sources."

"What was the case? Anything to do with Hawaii?"

He grunted, an inaudible language I had come to understand over the years. "They were shunting information back and forth primarily for safekeeping and it vanished."

"Jesus! No wonder they use the press so liberally. Any idea what the documentation had to do with?"

"Child abduction cases."

"Unbelievable. How much did this cost you?"

"Not a damn thing, but Avi —"

"I'm here." I could feel my energy revving up again.

"Play this down really cool. The guy's name is Clearspring. He's a cop on Oahu, and he's got the central thread on this kind of action."

"How do they talk about him?"

"He went under. He belongs to the other side."

"Maybe it's not a cover."

"And maybe he's waiting to blow half the police force away. Remember, there was a leak. Clearspring's not from the West coast. He's lived in the Islands his entire life."

"What was that about?" Libby asked with some irritation when I returned to the room.

"Don't worry. It's not love. I was talking to my editor."

"Since when do we keep secrets, babe?"

"What? You want my byline? I did a short paragraph on Lt. Honoka'a."

"I may as well tell you. They put us in a big fancy place because we aren't going after the primary lead."

"Could be he has money," I suggested, and borrowed a cigarette.

"Could be, my ass. These men are on the run from something. Whatever they were educated for, they aren't doing it. They are living by their wits on any dollar they can and they have eyes and ears halfway across the country advising them where the landmines are."

The tip had gone to my head. I reeled back to reality and sobered. "You live for this pace. I don't."

"Get used to it, angel. We're going to fan out all over the island tonight and go in with nighttime wear. We'll be in the dark all night."

It sounded like a threat. "Who invites you on these police investigations?"

"We've had an arrangement for the past ten years. What's theirs is ours. They get to call the timing of when we go to press."

"David gave me as much time as I need."

"Good." She got up and cleared the breakfast table and spread out a map of The Big Island, circling with a red grease pencil the base camp at Kona and the suspected camps throughout the island. "It's a bigger stretch than the other islands," she said. "With more room to hide. Also there's no satelitte capability here as there is on Kauai and Oahu, which means less detection."

"I went out to the Kau desert. I'm surprised they found detectable traces of sand in those pits."

"I'm surprised they lugged anything from the desert. It's hair brained." She took two beers out of the refrigerator and used a bottle opener on the wall to uncap them. She handed me one as she sat. "I've given alot of thought as to why this group split into subgroups. I think when they have management difficulties with kids' reactions they line up the problem kid with a sweetheart. I think the blond kid you saw is expected to go in to subdue a problem kid."

"I agree. I just think someone should've staked out where he was taken."

"Trust me, they did. Honoka'a doesn't let any lead get away. I also think they have their own boat. I don't think it's anchoring anywhere visible. A dinghy probably meets it and brings the children in."

"Have you told Kane?"

"I did, after we debriefed this morning. The other thing is no matter how old these children become, my guess is their body hair is shaved."

I took a few drags on my cigarette and exhaled. "You've figured out the psychology."

"I'm working on it."

"Have you talked to Laura Sojimoto?"

"I haven't talked to anyone. You're the first."

"What gave you the idea?"

"There are too many children not to rebel and —"

"Maybe they did rebel. Maybe that's the reason for the small groups and the horrific deaths."

"I didn't finish. I think these children are used to going naked. There was no body hair found in those gravesites. You would expect that with at least the older children."

"Not unless the graves were used for instruction or for young children. When does body start to grow?"

"I had to call someone in child development. She didn't know either. Her source told her in boys it's around age eleven."

I gaped. Recovering myself, I said, "Was the second child at Holo Holo Ku shaved?"

"It didn't grab my attention. He probably wasn't twelve yet."

"Or was a late bloomer."

Her face became implacable as her firmness of opinion asserted itself. "This particular ring does not appear to engage preteens who have begun to grow body hair. Also I don't think they use girls."

"I'm going to say they have both sexes. Have you given any thought to who obtained ketamine?"

She smiled slowly. I remembered the smile in Vietnam. We had returned to Ho Chi Minh City to consult a guide who spoke French and Mandarin. She was younger then, less embittered and the smile indicated something hit home. "The only type of person under God's green earth who would use ketamine is a veternarian. No one else would have access."

"How about an intern?"

She pulled back then, understanding there were a thousand ways to dice the onion. "Not a chance."

four

THE MEMBERS OF THE TEAM studied the aerial photographs of the Mauna Kea forested terrain taken by the reconnaissance A team. Several closeup camera shots had captured a clearing and a lineup of eights pits. The photos, shot at midnight by an extra terrestrial-manned spacecraft, showed no people nor activity. It looked like another tease game - we were here and now we're gone.

"We'll go in anyway," Kane said. "But only eight. If we encounter a suspect, I'll do the talking."

"I think sir with all due respect you have too much visibility. You were on television recently and in the news. To take them by surprise I think a team of greenhorns would be best."

There was no argument. The point was conceded to by the brass. It was agreed upon Libby and I would join six others, one who was a female detective for SWAT and that we would offer a pretense of being hikers. No two-tone grease nor fatigues. We also decided I would photograph. To make the most of it I'd carry a zoom and a flash.

We left at two in the afternoon.

"What do you think?" A Sergeant Ron Mathews asked, as the two dark green jeeps that carried us to the destination swerved to avoid pitted asphalt. He was tall, fairly good looking and the epitome of an outdoor enthusiast in color and muscle tone.

"I'm getting much more than I bargained for."

"I meant with reference to our network."

"You've got all bases covered."

He gave a terse nod. "We're moving on this as fast as we can, but our focus has longevity and memory, if you'll pardon the pun."

"Libby and I were both in Vietnam during the Cambodian crisis. I was a youngster, barely nineteen, but we camped in makeshift shacks and travelled in small bands by moonlight."

"They posted me in Germany during Nam," he said regretfully. "I wanted the front line but my superior officer felt I'd be better with transmissions."

"That was no secure post."

"No, but we didn't get bombed."

The jeeps rounded a bend. The road was covered by overhanging trees and lush green plants and vines which as we climbed in elevation reminded me more and more of a junle wilderness. Skin smooth moss covered the roadside and clung to the soil off steep ravines. From nowhere sprung into view waterfalls and rock surfaces, a myriad of patina-like colors in the sunlight, ledges rising through a shawl of greenery. As we approached the trailhead, the drops became more treacherous and ropelike vines dangled in thin air where they ought to remain connected to the undergrowth.

The jeeps parked on a patch of grass beneath leafy trees that nearly hid the two vehicles from sight. I set my camera for the degree of dappled light that filtered through the boughs. We started off on the trail, each of us carrying a backpack and roll and a water bottle and pouch with trail mix. The dirt path was covered with moss and damp stone and offered no real foothold for the uninitiated. They advanced as rock climbers would scaling the rock by firm handholds and walking sideways with feet pointed in each direction. A fall would be a goodbye kiss, so the group slowed to accomodate the nimblest climber. As we covered ground, a ledge thrust itself outward forming an overlook by which one could span the forest. Because we had only seen the area by aerial we were expecting the flat encampment to be about a quarter of a mile from the road. In actuality it was a half mile.

The air was cool but sticky and hard to breathe. I inhaled deeply to fill my lungs but the altitude defeated me, leaving me light-headed instead. I signalled to Libby who was having problems of her own. The cable she had brought was really meant as a hitch between two ledges and not for the rock face itself. She tried a spike but the rock face was tough without the soil or trees to fully support more than one person's weight. When we reached a part of the trail that led uphill over slickrock, she decided for the group the best plan was for she and one of the detectives to go ahead to determine the best method to get into the camp.

As we waited for the two to return we heard a child's voice come floating from below.

"I can't find it," the child said.

"Well, keep looking," replied an older male voice. "Remember what I told you about sticking to the perimeter."

"How am I supposed to do that with my eyes closed?"

I stepped over the rock until I could see to the ground some two hundred feet below. The child had to be seven, if that. He had dark blond hair and wore fatigues and a windband. I tried to discern whether he carried a weapon but the angle of my glance made it impossible to tell.

At length Libby returned with the detective. We backed up some fifty yards to the ledge and huddled.

"The path is steep over two narrow waterfalls with several hundred foot drops," she said. "We appear to be right above their camp."

"I counted two adults and four children," the detective said. "No one seems armed but I wouldn't want to risk my safety not knowing."

Another detective felt the ones who could should take the path while the other two or three dropped a rope to ground level.

Libby ditched the idea saying our cover would be blown if anyone were watching. We didn't have far to go, she asserted. We decided we would traverse uphill.

The stone path was at once bumpy and wet. The slickrock afforded little advantage. Almost immediately we dropped the idea of cinching the rope between us. As the path narrowed to a foot wide and the drop became more exaggerated, we took to moving sideways like cut-out paper figures. We followed the course through the waterfalls which flowed at intervals due to the lack of water. Moss and root tendrils clung to the wet soil where rock surface protruded. In time we came to the end of the path.

It opened onto a hillside. Five trenches had been built and had iron grates across them. Each trench was about two feet across by four feet long and two feet deep and appeared used to bake food. Two stayed behind and four of us moved down the hill to a knoll on which stood a rudimentary house made of boards and a grass roof. A fire burned in a pit approximately a hundred yards away. On the far side of the knoll were the pits we had seen in the aerial shots. Because the aerial should have picked up the shack, we weren't certain the pits seen in the nighttime photos were the ones we were looking at.

"May I help you?" A fairly nondescript man in his early forties came from the house. He was five foot nine inches, with brunnette hair that covered a slightly round head like a pudding, and appeared by his brisk manner and confidence to be in excellent physical shape.

The lead detective said, "We may be lost. We came in expecting to meet up with another party."

"No one here but us and the fleas. You bring a map? Maybe I can help."

Libby withdrew a map. She unfolded the map and pointed to the area which on the map appeared south of the camp.

"No such place," he said. "This is the only camp off this trail. Nearest trail is another two thousand feet up above us."

"Thanks. We're sorry to have bothered you."

"No bother."

Then Libby said, "You don't have a telephone by any chance?"

He eyed her. "You're in the Hawaiian wilderness, lady. No water pumps, no phones."

"Sorry," she said.

"It's alright."

We walked out half expecting the man to come at us with a rifle, mowing us down with bullets. But he didn't and we walked back this time in barefeet to give us a more secure foothold, our shoes and socks slung around our necks as balancing weights.

S AREVJO," KANE SAID, after the sketch artist completed the rendition of the man's face. "I recognize him from a bulletin that came across my desk half a million years ago."

He had dinner waiting for us in a conference room upon our return to King Hamehameha Hotel in Kona. The setting sun shimmered on the blue water. The last tourists who had stayed the day at the pool got up and came inside, highballs and sunglasses in hand.

We laughed over the notion there could be any coincidence which would make the case seem easier than it had been and gulped down roast duckling with iced tea. Libby was the life of the party. Between mouthfuls she told and retold about the sinewy ledges, the narrow footpath and ludicrous moment of finding ourselves face to face with a man who had to be the asshole of the century, let alone a pedophile or ax murderer and us having no ability to obtain more information or see inside the hut.

The sketch artist fed the final picture into the fax machine. We decided that when Leavenworth came through with a name and last known whereabouts, another night would've passed and very possibly another day. The sitting around would be the worst, like awaiting a jury's decision after a long unyielding case. When the print hammer knocked out the criminal history if there was any, we'd be ready for tranquilizers and mood elevators.

I'm placing you in protective custody," Kane told a furious Libby waking us both in the middle of the night to inform us they had penetrated the man's identity. "You covered a case involving him."

"What the hell was it?" She sputtered, not fully awake and feeling cheated in the big moment.

"On the rain forests. He was residing outside the Koh Forest in Seattle. You got him on film."

"He probably never saw me face to face," she complained.

"We can't take the risk. Plus when we go back in we aren't taking anyone but ourselves in. If he doesn't come quietly —"

"He'll move camp," she said in defiance of him and then remembering what had occurred on the case she said, "He was a reconn expert in the war."

"Was he there when you two were?"

"I've never seen him before," I said.

"You'll be doing us a favor," Kane said to her. "You'll be

going in on the Inside for thirty hours."

"What the fuck for?" She exploded. "I won't be able to write this story if my sources all can be identified. Why can't you send in someone else?"

"Because," he said with a grin, "I'm handing you a caveat."

"Put me in," I suggested.

"Nothing doing. I'm taking you home to my mother's."

If experience tells all and truth is a lousy second, the minute Libby got out she'd be on every wire in the city. Whatever Lt. Honoka'a had set into motion, I decided I'd better be ready since he had chosen me to pick up the pieces. It was an interesting dance, to simultaneously be handed an integral lead and nothing at all and then boxed into a corner.

I had accompanied Libby into the jail, watched her get fingerprinted and mugged, then escorted down a series of locking corridors past Command Central, handed over to another guard and led to the women's section of the hundred and two bed jail. I noticed the woman who lay on the bed in the cell next to Libby's; she was medium height, golden hair to her shoulders, a scowl that probably was her one defense against pickups, and scars of cuts and bruises on her neck and hands. The woman stared through me. There was something that wasn't right about her. The eyes looked straight at me without seeing me and her voice when she asked when her time would be up was soothing and menacing at the same time, a sound one wanted to unhear. There was something else also, something that said she had been tortured or used by men, or subjected to evil and that she knew what it had done to her and what it did to people who did not understand what it could do.

After I hugged Libby goodbye, the woman turned to me and laughed. It was malicious laughter. I knew what Libby was thinking. She had had no real sleep and wouldn't react well to another woman's mocking laughter. I think Libby was in a mood to rip the woman's eyes out of her face.

Quenan had dinner waiting. Kane washed his hands in the wash basin outside on the back porch so as not to interfere with his mother's kitchen while I reviewed my notes and put in a call to the West coast. The meal consisted of glazed pork chops, poi, stewed apples, broccoli and yams, and tea. Over dinner we chatted about Kane's father.

"I forgot to tell my husband I loved him but he loved me so much it was okay."

I smiled happily like a child, fed on real relationships.

He had taken her to England one summer and her experience of it was morbid. "If ever in England visit the north coast but be wary of the caves. It's where they tested detonations."

"I thought they were getting rid of empty spaces," he said, to humor her.

"They were getting rid of vultures." And then, as though amused by his joke in retrospect she said, "The suburb costs less than the water. Of course the village is least expensive because no one shall ever tell. The orchard unfortunately is a fortune - it never pays for itself." To me, "If you stay long enough, get all that is grown here and you'll be rich and healthy. Do you get paid for what you do?"

"I work six months out of the year and freelance the rest. As an independent I am paid $25,000."

She mulled this over, chewing the last meat on the pork chop. "I suppose if you're lucky it's $28,000."

"I often spend a good deal on expenses to get in close."

She eyed Kane who replied, "They never say no twice. Sometimes a journalist gets it on the first admission."

"I learned the hard way I had to omit the sensational in writing."

"Speaking of learning what will this article tell you?"

"That I don't ever want to grow old. That things change too much and that I've resisted changing. Getting on in one's years, past one's prime, is difficult."

Quenan cleared the table and brought out a good Jewish lemon cake and made a calming tea.

We talked into the night. Her mother was originally from Sweden. She had a half sister on her mother's side from a first marriage who was older than she was who was born in 1903 and grew up in Sweden. The first war took her father. He never returned - whole or any other way. She married by 1925 at age 24. She joined the war effort and flew into Germany through the Netherlands in 1932, was captured in 1933 when her plane was reported shot down, held two months and released. In 1938 she came to Hilo where she lived until after the war, then joined the orchid business.

She said, "Jenna still speaks the Swedish language. She will tell you she feels destroyed without her husband and that Frank O'Connor was her most admired writer."

I kept pace until Kane said goodnight. Then the weariness of the day leaked out of me driving me to clear the dishes off the table. Quenan wouldn't hear of it. She said there were too few days when one lived like a king and we'd leave the desert table for the flies until morning.

THE HIRED HAND who drove me into town told me of all the adjustments the islanders had to do, the worst was that the drinking water was getting killed off on the more remote islands.

He told me Libby had taken him on a trip a few years ago to Equador to do a story on the El Oro oil company which forced the Cofan Indians to move. The military had come in instead of the Catholic church to become defacto owners of the land. They had found the rivers polluted and the wildlife had run off. Seventeen million gallons of oil had spilled into Lago Abria causing cancer, deformities, diahrrea and sponta-neous abortion. Lago Abria was where the Indians drank, ate and fished.

Armed confrontations with oil had led to village massa-cres. When oil arrived with seismic equipment and bright lights for night work, the military had to bring arbitrators to file injunctions to stop the drilling. He said he thought she covered important news. I said I thought so too.

I flew with Kane to the Big Island to the Hawaii County Library on Waianuenue Avenue. Someone had overturned the Naha stone which was one of two museum pieces that stood in front of the library. Hawaii legend had it that the person who could move the stone would become king of the island and the person who overturned it would conquer all the islands. King Hamehameha was the last person to over-turn it.

Officer Lee met us at the Hilo airport. He was convinced this act was a development to the case. He called it, the no one is laughing stone.

The call had come in that morning at 4:45am and it was now four hours later. A line of patrol vehicles, their lights flashing, had cordoned off the area. Lee parked, and we pushed our way through the crowd that had gathered. The stone looked to be a good half ton and was splashed liberally with red paint or animal blood.

"Any idea how it was overturned?" Kane asked Lee.

Lee shrugged. "Someone saw someone resembling Clearspring with a pair of renegades arrive with a crane. Where they came from," he added, anticipating the question, "is anyone's guess."

An officer came over to us and asked us to step aside. We did, as the forensic team with hydraulic water power arrived to hose off the museum piece.

The blast of water was ear piercing, a trauma of light and sound to rock a person's internal morbidity. I escaped to a canteen where I purchased a cup of coffee for fifty cents and watched from a distance.

The fact that the rock had been overturned without being overheard by surrounding neighbors indicated they possibly thought they were hearing a typical city sound such as a street sweeper or towing truck. The effort taken by a bunch of hoodlums struck me not as sacrilegious as I knew some writer would likely comment but as a waste of time. Imagining they had come out in the night to surprise a staff of library clerks was one thing, but my guess was whoever had done this wanted to suggest they could move heaven or hell to get back at the ever growing numbers of investigators arriving to join the rotation for on duty detectives.

Kane joined me. He bought a cup of coffee for himself also and stood sipping it. "There was a note attached. It read, 'Why not drop this on a man's head?'"

"Any idea what this is really about?"

"We run a refugee camp out near the hydroelectric plant," he said flatly. "It's where you get sovereignty as a headliner. We figure if you know how the story reads then you're supposed to know and if you don't know, then it's information you weren't meant to know."

"What is a refugee camp?"

"It's a modern day prison system which actually is quite ancient. A branch of government tracks criminals who we know we can't bring in through detention and the court system. Either the evidence won't stand up to legal standards or rebuttal isn't strong enough or they have produced an unbreakable alibi. Once this branch of law hones in on who the criminals are the particular federal officers persuade them to relocate to particular housing developments. The housing development over time becomes a refugee camp."

"And?" I asked, still not getting the entire picture.

"And we punish them depending upon the severity of the crime."

"What if a person escapes, goes to another country?"

"The United Nations handles people who escape. Every last country has the same system in place."

"Which crimes are punished?"

"Bombings, arson, embezzlement, theft, burglary, molestation, assaults of every kind both on an officer or the law or of the peace and citizens, computer hacking, and quasi crimes."

"Such as?"

"Hacking up someone's water pipes so that in event of a problem their sprinkler system is permanently disabled."

"As in a fire. I got it. What else?"

"Soliciting sex from underage minors, signing up a family member without their knowledge for death insurance, purposefully running into another person's vehicle in order to increase services of insurance such as auto repair or medical services, performing surgery on people who don't require the surgery and purposely misdiagnosing someone for profit. There's more but I can't think of them at the moment."

"That's a good system of justice."

"We think so too. Over time you feel you can actually recoup a sense of safety in the world at large."

"Do you explain this to the suspect?"

"When they are broke. When we have them cornered. When we have direct evidence such as their photograph on a closed circuit or a friend or witness comes forward. Well?"

"I think you're braver than I am."

We stood and sipped our coffee. The hydraulic truck had completed its task. It was doubtful whether a crane would be called to ressurect the stone into its previous position. As the truck pulled away, officers inserted stakes and rolled out caution tape.

At length Kane said, "Try writing the sovereignty article from another point of view. Talk about Cambodian refugees finding sanctions on the island."

I gave an appreciative nod. "What about this team of pedophiles and their victims. You don't take the children, do you?"

I would have trouble sleeping, I decided as my mind kept returning to a sound on the porch of one of the houses on the Honoka'a orchid farm that reminded me of whiplash. The fact that sometimes children could not be separated from a criminal parent or the parent in finally comprehending what type of justice they had to face had had a child to evade the punishment overwhelmed me.

I had left Libby who had stayed over to use my laptop to transfer half a dozen articles she had researched into my data files. The hills were lush green, the valley also was a swathe of green. On the Big Island someone was rocking the cradle, giving birth to yet another episode of passing. I recapitulated to some god I wasn't sure was out there what I had taken away with me from the morning - it was neither about justice nor about greed. I was angry there were people who committed crimes, who were motivated by some non existant idea of easy street or who didn't care what meanness they subjected the innocent to.

Do you remember the boat that took us into Vietnam?" Libby asked, as she rolled a cigarette and then tamped it and lit it.

I nodded. "I thought we were going to get fucked. All those big wheel tires, stacks and stacks of coca cola bottles, fortresses of tennis shoes and that crazy man who slept at the door with a string of bullets around his neck at the ready for the men who busted out of their cages."

"That's what's going on here. You have to go back ten to twelve years for the crimes the adults committed. They raised the children, had children with their children and then repeated crimes including murdering the older children. This group has been tracked for as long as they've been on the run. It's sick; it's depressing, but you're a big girl now and can stand to hear the truth."

I took her cigarette and she rolled herself another. "It feels like there is nothing to live for."

"You snap out of it eventually. You step back from your own life and after rethinking it all find yourself travelling to see how the same hat is worn in different countries."

"Tien drove me in this morning. He said you'd gone to Nicaragua."

"No, it was Equador. I ran into a little problem there. A group of men had built a shelter and were allegedly making a movie, but the actual truth was they'd arranged their own funerals after blowing up a sugarcane plant in Alabama and were holding back the tribes with handguns and heavy artillery.

"It's a catch-22," she said, and took a drag on her cigarette. "Take the swing hammer here, the mechanism that produces the whiplash sound you hear coming from the closet. That's the first stage. The second is they produce a laboratory setting inside the residence and interfere with your sleep. Sounds startle the criminal out of sleep, he smells smoke, the faucet doesn't work right, eventually nothing can be replaced, sometimes the punishing crew lets the plumbing but turns on the heating and doesn't shut it down. It can go from bad to worse.

"I married my husband because I felt I was lagging behind in my life. I wanted a nicer house than what I could afford to give myself. He purchased the better half of the condo, let me buy expensive furniture on his white plastic before I learned he was an insider trader in his job as a stockbroker. It shocked me. Then he had the automobile accident that left him crippled and eventually I took it in that you can't have everything. Believe me, I didn't want to arrive at that sorry conclusion but that's where the airplane set me down."

I had always admired her and she knew it. I had wanted her life and she knew that too. I suppose it came as a relief for her to realize I'd never catch up to what she had aquired through her marriage. Some losses were too great. Some stole your life even as you lived.

"I think about that first boatride in," she said, pensive now. "There were no bodies nor evidence of war. Yet there was a hundred percent crime. All that beauty and so much terror."

"The story will take shape, don't worry," I said.

"I know your mind doesn't return there the way mine does. The second war was a bad one. We weren't alive then, but I'm told it's why Hawaii remains in the sugarcane export business. We walk them back and forth to Vallejo and the C&H factory to assure ourselves they aren't going to try to bomb us again."

"I didn't realize the Japanese came through Hawaii to the mainland."

"Well, no one says so but the ones who tried to blow up

the naval kitchens at Concord came from somewhere."

"I think that was the excuse we needed to shut down the coast."

"Talk to Quenan when you have nothing better to do. Get her to tell you about being stationed at Napa waiting for ship orders."

I smiled as I exhaled. If Quenan told me about the cost of refugee camps, it was as much as I'd ever hear unless I quit my job and stayed. "You going to write an article on this stuff?"

"My editor told me what she wanted before you had flown out. The movies were meant to help the wannabe criminal acclimate. Instead the adventure movies replaced the sadistic images that came with dream suspension with socially accepted ways to channel the need for sudden wealth. It was supposed to be the wannabe couldn't stomach what they saw and turned away from it out of moral goodness."

"You won't write that. I wouldn't."

"The pedophiles applied for a movie permit. It's how they got here."

"I'm interested in going after them. Can you get me in on the A-team?"

I WATCHED THROUGH binoculars at the running man. He was thin, little more than medium height, dark hair, dressed in lightweight windbreaker material which rippled against his body as he ran. He ran barefoot over bassaltic cliffs, as the verdant emerald mountains rose behind him. I could tell he was long used to the regimen because he had been running at this speed for almost an hour. In places where the spongy mantel of grass dipped he manuevered himself pulling in his arms and propelling himself with the speed of an underwater swimmer. He travelled with confidence until the ground reasserted itself causing him to adjust and with more directness charge forward.

I'd decided he was older than the five or so other men I'd glimpsed at the camp. If he was in his late thirties or early forties he had long ago made peace with age and minor losses of agility through this dedication to discipline. He had sorted through the melodramas one goes through with breathing, reaching that point where the air becomes too thin and the body fights the urge to slow down to compensate. He got away from the tension or the tightness created by whatever his task was at the camp.

I had spent the night listening to Kane repeating sounds into a megaphone and hearing them come back and then recording the sharpness of breath onto a casette recorder. *KA-nee, KA-ee, NOO-ee, COW-cow MY-kye.* Or roughly The ocean, the big ocean brings plentiful food. He talked of the marlin, tuna and mahi mahi caught at hukilaus with his father, brothers, unlces and grandfather, and of lomilomi salmon baked in a kalua, or underground oven. He took a break to tell me he was not so old that he had forgotten the meaning of words like *'ohana* for clan group or *mo'opuna*, for grandchildren or *kama'aina*, for native born. Nor so old to have forgotten how to choose the right tree for a canoe tree or to fit the proportions and curves of the canoe into the tree as one was carving it.

Quenan left as he was explaining what his father used to say, that a good canoe tree stood a straight fifty feet tall and was four feet thick. A perfect tree, he said, wasn't that hard to find but today since Hawaii had become a state, craftspeople had to adapt, look for trees in deep ravines, and trim away rot and fungus before hollowing out the tree. He felt the koa canoe made from the koa tree when compared to canoes made from fiberglass was something to respect because it came from something that was once living, not from artificial material put together in a factory.

This was such a man, I thought as I watched him come down toward the valley floor without reducing his speed. It made him dangerous, because without checks on the mental superiority he probably felt he possessed he probably expected to run the camp; if not this one, then the ones where the young teens resided. I zeroed in on his face and adjusted the sight until I had him visibly before me. He was handsome and hard at the same time, unflinching in his movement, coming down the trail at four miles an hour or faster, needing neither to slow to accommodate dangling roots or open guava skins, the speed taking every possible fall or misstep into account.

Fog descended with him and mist, one moment impervious to drizzle, in the next minute became a damp rain. He ran sideways, holding himself tightly as though on a rein, borrowing against natural erosion created by bark and leaves and soil. I admired his deftness as he showed through the foliage, cresting as it were as the trail seemed to take yet another swell, then angling beneath hanging moss and soft elms as he made for the camp.

I scouted out the dimensions of the camp, sketching in charcoal the perimeters of the mountain pass that surrounded the base camp. Then a separate sketch of the camp itself and of the circular trail outlets. Then I shot a roll of thirty-six closeups and marked in a notepad directions and landmarks.

I followed Libby into the rotunda of the state capitol building and we found Officer Lee standing beneath a painting by Americo Makk studying the dark colors and intense light that made the picture a stark portrayal of Indians around an abandoned campfire. We took the elevator to the second floor and walked to the end of the hall to a conference room from where state and now federal bureaus were coodinating their investigations. A photographic lineup of the kidnapped youths along with sketch guesses of who they now were lined one wall. Files were everywhere, stacked in files on long tables, on desks, on the floor. At the back was a network of computers hooked up to several printers which hammered out transmissions on a seemingly endless flow of paper.

It was 0700 hours. The A-team was mulling over aerial shots along with dozens of black and white glossies taken of youths on the streets and of two camps, both situated in the wilds of the Big Island.

Dr. Laura Sojimoto explained as we pulled up chairs and I handed over the clips I had taken. "They're interrogating a man named Johnson," she began, and shot his photograph over the table into Officer Lee's hands. I recognized him as the man who we'd come across when we made the raid on the first camp.

"Several significant developments occurred after as a result of the Naha stone we circulated APBs on the teens we spotted. The first was this man you see here moved from the place the team found him to here," and tapped an isolated spot near the hydroelectric plant. "Second, we were shown, we think because the maneuvering to get us there appeared so deliberate, to one of the beach camps on the northwest side of the island nearest the state park. We came across a group of approximately nine young children, between ages six to ten, many of whom look very primitive and undersocialized.

"This could be owing of course to the fact that their parents or families abandoned them or they were sold to several adults as slaves. Their accommodations are less than adequate; most are sleeping on bedrolls in sleeping bags."

"At least they aren't graves," Libby put in quickly.

"Are they clothed?" Someone else asked.

"Fully," Laura answered. "They aren't wanting for clothing nor for shoes. If they have access to church bins or periodic shelters, they're doing okay in that respect. It's their demeanor. They seem to be in a daze, or worse - semi psychotic."

"They're probably fine, just hungry or having survived by their wits for too long," Libby said, too defiantly and we all got wind of an objection she had with the psychological labeling that could affect these children in the future.

Officer Mike Lee said, somewhat contritely, "Do we expect their parents to return for them?"

"Well that's it, we don't know." She said, and deferred to Kane.

He sat on his chair backwards. "We learned of the wilderness camps by accident. We picked up movement when one of the flares went down. That's where you went," he said to me. "The other we picked up by accident when we tried to match the particulars to the one we did find. At this one we discovered after pouring over the aerials that they have refrigeration. They appear to be taking blood samples and spinning them down, possibly to create serums."

"For themselves?"

"We think they may have acquired rare diseases as a result of their living styles."

"Or perhaps the adults have diseases and they require the children available for testing." The forensic specialist who had attended said. "Maybe that's the reason the children died. Their bodies were unable to tolerate the level of saturation and they stopped breathing."

Everyone looked with vivid interest at her.

"Perhaps the child whose head we found developed another problem. Perhaps he, or she, developed leprosy or cancer which became invasive —"

"Into the bone," Kane said, agreeing. "And the child whose neck was cut?"

"Could be the child went insane and cut his own throat. Of course it doesn't explain the lack of coagulation we found and can't explain."

"Why? What would you expect?" Someone asked.

"Very little bubbling of the blood and no gushing. Normally the body instantly coagulates as a defense against infection. The blood does not remain thin."

"What do you think that means?"

"We don't have any idea," said Dr. Sojimoto.

"We want the adults from the camp where the runner is from," Kane interjected. "When we have them in cuffs, when we know from them who the children and teens are, then we'll send rescues for them as well."

Libby removed a pack of cigarettes, got up and went over to the balcony as she lit a cigarette. "Any idea how dangerous these men are?"

"None whatsoever." Kane told her.

"Because I find this serum stuff terrifying. What happens if you go in and don't make it out? What happens if they need more than other people's blood? If they require safe subjects to inject their blood into to test how to purify whatever disease they're looking to get rid of?

"You have no concept of reality here, none." She said, her voice raising with fear. "No idea of limits here. These must be desperate people especially if the adults were criminals and have been hunted down to the islands. Especially as a result of living without plumbing and being exposed to continual damp they caught plague or pneumonia or some other damning illness such as leprosy."

Laura and Kane conceded the point. Laura said, "My own preference is to go in one at a time and wire the camp so escape is impossible and then motivate them to leave such as with a fire."

Libby countered, "My preference is to drop vials of blood and see if they leave the children alone."

"We aren't going to do that," Kane said. "And we aren't in a position to send in a scout to pretend to be one of them to try to get these teens to leave with him. For one thing I don't think these teens would leave with anyone. They're probably in a frozen state of terror."

"Then send me and Avi in. We did a tour of duty in Nam. We can handle this."

"If they move, we're in trouble," Kane warned.

"We'll have you train with a pro for a forty-eight hour period," said Honolulu's Captain Necker who arrived for a session with military lieutenants that was to follow this meeting.

The group turned to acknowledge him. He was a stocky man with blue eyes and wavy sandy hair.

"We'll stick you on the base for buildup and timing and trust me, unless you've been sitting in a sauna munching fried mackerel, you'll be ready for any baloney they hand you."

∧∧∧

Through binoculars the camp was sparse and unsettling. The runner slept outside beneath the stars. A man each was posted in a tent made of nylon at the perimeters of the camp. Two men slept inside a makeshift house which by the aid of a reconn scope was determined to lack insulation although it contained drywall and electric outlets. If serology tests were conducted at this site, during the day the men appeared not to be engaged in them. Instead they tended to vegetables they were growing, zuccinis and cucumbers and lettuce, applying what looked to be some kind of soupy mixture. Libby shot the pictures and I took measurements and reproduced the camp onto picturebook size sheets with a legend and a ruler. Between sips of gatorade-spiked water, dried salami sticks and nuts, we conducted surveillance.

The men in the camp weren't going anywhere, we decided as we bedded down on foam rolls beneath shamoi covers and smoked a cigarette between us. This camp was meant as a lookout or a point of entry, and although the aerials didn't show any connecting trail, there had to be one. In whispers we gave ourselves tasks which we would complete the next day — move closer to camp, take a straw poll as to how much of the surrounding vegetation might be edible, try to determine what the soup was made of.

I took the first shift while Libby slept for two hours. Then it was my turn. We piggybacked two hours sleep each until morning. At daybreak we were both awake and had buried all evidence of our gear except our food.

I braced myself for the heat that bathed me in sweat as I ran a course up the hillside above the trail the runner from the camp utilized. The high altitude cut the air. I pushed the windband over my nose and mouth forcing me to take in reduced air. The ground was dry but without the leaves or squishy fruit that made the last trail I had taken treacherous. Branches slapped my face and lush leafy plants brushed my arms as I slipped into an easy gait moving with minimum effort. My feet stayed with confidence, the mountain seemed to try me with the effort of history as though a hundred years ago the size of the island lay flatter and more receptive to vanquished men who set about to make one room cabins on the edge of the water. Below, although I was unable to see him, the man moved also with confidence, a graceful runner who was seeking to conquer time or endurance, or something in between. I could almost sense the training he had given himself like tiny sips taken more for the fact that hard air tenses the muscles and must surely deplete the body's ability to manufacture whatever releases promote ease. He had no strain as he ran up the elevation. As he crested at the elevation where my trail dropped twenty or so feet I glimpsed him. He was sleek with firm well practised muscles but without sweat. If he had to push against some sort of envelope as I did, he had travelled the path so often he knew when to slow, when to increase speed and how much air to take in.

He had the advantage as he descended at the downturn and tucked in his chin and somewhat bowed his knees. I slid and went down, landing on my fanny, scraping the dirt, leveraging myself with my palms. The path was steeper than I'd expected. I exhaled and then as I drew in breath the air clamped and I realized if I did not stand I would lose momentum. I stood and still running tumbled, clutching as I fell at whatever plants might offer an anchor but they detached readily from the soil. I got up again and this time I did what the runner did, bowlegging my body and slowing almost to a moderate walk. The runner sensed me as I feared he might and paused just long enough for me to fear we could collide. I ignored both fear and caution and kept moving suppressing my breath until he took flight a moment later and ran now to make up for the hesitation caution produced in him.

The path I was on dipped and turned and wound above thin waterfalls. Mist lifted and wet, purple and yellow flowering plants decended cascading between rock faces, insinuating between swells and depressions. When I discovered I could see the sea I turned back several hundred yards and using tendril vines as ropes and a spike to steady my weight I lowered myself through the garden wilderness. A light spray caught my face and I turned, careful not to alter the gradual descent in any way, stabbing the soil with the spike, drawing each vine to me as my shoes found enough of a hold to steady myself. As the waterfall receded into the rock I used the split rock face for my hands and moved slowly downward, negotiating with my weight for clefts in the rock to support my shoes. At the trail I jumped landing unsteadily and shifted my body taking the next down cline in a run.

I would be behind the runner now. Not knowing the path nor where it exited into the camp, I slowed. As the trees thinned and I could see clearly that the vegetation had been stripped from the trail I slid off the path onto the leaf covered soil and descended sideways. Dried leaves caused me to slip and I went down shoes forward until I came to the edge of camp.

The runner sat on a burlap folding chair. Another man was drawing vials of blood. When he had three vials he unsnapped the tourniquet and removed the needle and inserted the needle into a needle cutter and crunched the needle. The glass syringe was tossed into a sudsy solution. I watched as the man who had taken the blood stepped into a cabin. Through the open door I could see him spin the vials down in a centrifuge, then light a bunsen burner, drop blood by use of a dropper onto several plates and cultures and then heat the remaining blood. I shot as many photos as I dared to take with a small hand-held camera. They were insane I thought and inched back up the flank of the hill to the path. If they had contracted a deadly poison or worse, experimented with ways to prolong life or alter DNA, the measures they could undertake could get them killed.

Then I thought of the children. I became angry realizing that these men, once they thought they had a serum, were in all probability injecting their children. It accounted for the deaths, for the unexplained plasma changes the forensic staff were seeing, for problems in coagulation, for the impulsive act with the Naha stone as though the library with its sumptive knowledge contained everything but the scientific protocols as to how to reverse toxins and disease. As I stood and propelled myself into a slow run up the trail and felt its demands on my body, I wondered how on earth these adults got themselves with a group of kidnapped preteens to this reality. I wondered who they were and what they had done prior to kidnapping children and hiding out like a bunch of wild beasts on a handful of islands. I felt this discovery contained more urgency than even saving the two groups of children.

We broke down camp, packed up and got out while it was night. I told Libby when we'd made it back safely to her jeep rental that I thought we were dealing with a handful of seriously motivated perpetrators and not simply with a kidnapping ring or with cybersex junkies who were handing children over to pedophiles. She pulled over to the shoulder of the road, turned on the overhead light and flipped through my sketchbook.

"These are good, Avi," she said, after a silence. "We'll stop in to Kane and have him run these through as faxes for comparison." Then, lighting a cigarette and inhaling deeply, she said, "They aren't Hawaiian, are they? These men?"

"No. Possibly Hispanic or maybe some mix."

She took another drag. "They're a mining outfit out of Honduras. I recognize him," she said, rapping the sketch with her knuckles of her left hand. "He was the one the corporations sent in to lock up villagers and then burn their houses with gasoline before they brought in the tractors to cut down the forest. He's no spring chicken. He's a good sixty-three years old."

"He doesn't look it," I said, and then wondered aloud, "What do you make of this? Are they barricading themselves out here, or what?"

She smoked the cigarette to the filter. "I'll tell you this. Whatever I saw when I went to De Oro, it wasn't legal. I must've been looking at a standoff and no one wanted to call it for what it was, at least not with me there."

The photographs Kane produced from classified military files showed the two men viewed by me along with three others we had seen in and about Kona. They were dark enough to pass for Hawaiian but could also pass for Central or South American or Mediterraneum. Although they appeared in their late thirties, Libby's photo shots taken from her trip to Central America revealed them to be at least in their late fifties if not early sixties. Their youthfulness was accounted for perhaps by blood compotes or by steroids or by interacting predominantly with children and preteens. In wilderness camps inaccessible by the genral public they might live forever undetected or if seen in an aerial, unidentified or perceived to be too young a set.

The overhead light burned with the intensity of the hour. We sat bleary eyed fortifying ourselves with coffee that caused us to appear wired and poured over Libby's notes and the slowly thick file we were building on who these men had to be. Two were brothers; the other three had travelled as young men seeking their fortunes to work for a mine with an American-based corporation. No one expected any trouble but after the village was burned, the oil wells were punctured and a steady and thick stream of oil flowed into the ocean and killed off fish and drinking water. It was a fuck-you note of the century, canoes sank, wild boars dead of poison, and fields of forests in every direction burning as though a volcano had lit up the night sky and spilled ash over the land. Outlying villages lost their crops, families went blind and children developed huge canker sores that were unresponsive to any treatment.

"Who do you think these men burned forests for?" I asked.

"You mean, did they leach the oil from the refineries?" Libby said, redefining the problem. "The corporations retaliated. Yes, I think it's possible. I think these men did it to bolster the economy that was already there."

"Which was?"

"Coffee, Avi. We pay a steep price for a product no one wants to see continue to go up in price. To wind up paying for it at the cost many of these communities want to live involves a radical change in lifestyle. They might as well grow tobacco but there isn't a market for it anywhere in the world, no matter how many packs a day I smoke."

We laughed. Kane had called his son twice during the night. He now produced a lineup of beached ships parked permanently in the bays and told us that was where the problems were. These men had torpedoed the ballasts sinking half and stolen the plates to produce Argentinian legal tender to pay for the labor they would accommodate over the next five or so years. Better to have the money than to have to recreate a government after the Americanos departed to sustain the trade.

Disillusionment clobbered me at two in the morning and I retracted myself into a study to curl up on a divan. I closed the door on Libby's and Kane's discussion as to chronology of events and fell into a deep sleep. Before dawn I awoke. My legs ached with the running I had put myself through. I found a towel on the table at the foot of the bed and tiptoed across the hall to the shower. I passed Kane's room where I glimpsed him curled up like a spoon around Libby's thin body. The door to the son's room was closed but I suspected the young man I'd seen wandering around the police station was at a friend's during the final hours of the investigation. Where she got the nerve to enter into relationships so readily was a question which as I closed the bathroom door and ran the water for a shower faded as I realized they had probably worked together for years on any number of cases. I had liked him myself and failed to act on it or had not been given the chance because he wanted her or wanted someone he lived near.

In a day or two I'd be leaving and all this insanity would

be behind me. I'd be facing a stack of correspondence on my desk and a new assignment. It'd be easy come, easy go.

THE CHILD IN the nursery had a rash on both hands. He had been picked up on the beach scantily clothed, his upper lip split and opening like a cleft palate surgery which had failed or not been completed successfully. He was blond, quiet looking, a waif. He was the youngest of his group judging by the seven other children who had rashes on other parts of their bodies, a face, arms, upper chest, inner thigh, legs and knees, ankles and feet. Also one child had an unsteady gait, another possessed a limp, and several had somewhat caved in chests. Not unlike orphans we'd seen huddled together outside an unofficial U.S. Information Services in the Mekong delta feeding on small bowls of rice noodles and corn. They too seemed oddly aged, dispossessed of youth and certainly of semblance to modern children who attended city or private schools including in rural tracts.

I had a hard time looking at them. Libby fidgetted with a cigarette as she spoke into a hand held casette recorder noting occasional drooling, stupor, age inappropriate languidness or snoring. Periodically a psychologist or student entered the observation room and after watching for fifteen minutes left. I left short of an hour.

"Makes you nervous, doesn't it?" Libby asked, following me.

"My editor wants me to focus exclusively on the para military style camps, provide photographs of the graves, areas for washing and sleeping as well as lookouts."

"That's a good article. He has some good direction, your David."

I gave a nod. "Your city desk wants a real humdinger from you. You up for it?"

"After Sam's paralysis, nothing much fazes me."

We were standing in a normally crowded hall which was empty except for us. "You going to ask me about Kane?"

"I'm surprised, Lib."

"It'll be over in a few months."

We walked toward the blue door and the elevator to the second floor.

"What does Sam think about your affairs?" I asked. "Or does he care?"

"He's not in a position to say much. My resentment comes and goes. He's no longer a sexual partner and I'm too young to sit around."

"But why Kane?"

"Well," she said, and bent to light a cigarette, "it just happened. One minute we were talking about memory loss as a result of severe trauma and the next he took my hand and placed it on his leg. I don't need much in the way of encouragement. Anyway I waited because I thought he liked you."

"No, there's nothing there."

"Will you see Quenan before you leave?"

"Oh definitely. I have to develop my photographs, organize my notes. That'll take a day. Then I want to talk to the forensics team for their input and if I need to take a jaunt to photograph the quarantine group of kids. They're older, they may remember more."

"Kane gave you the go-ahead?"

I detected stirrings of jealousy. "I didn't ask him. I spoke to Captain Necker."

"I've got an idea," she said as we walked to the street and

across it, to the newly set up offices of the federal bureau of investigators and psychologists who would be taking over. The sky was clear. There was a faint sultry wind. "This crime was conceived when the rain forest was cleared in the Seventies to begin harvesting balsa. My belief is corporations wanted to isolate west from east and ran into a multitude of difficulties figuring out how to situate furniture and shipping production closer in from Asia."

Always the thinker. I said, "It has to be a frightening proposition after a hundred years to cut loose a continent."

"It's driven by practicality. Asia and Russia have too many impenetrable mountains. The Americas are relatively flat."

She opened the door for me in the four story building with smoke tinted windows. We stepped into a cool, luxuriously dark green carpeted hall with gold framed oil paintings depicting the East coast in winter. We rode the elevator to the second floor, then walked to the office of a child development specialist.

"Avi, this is Nicola Richlieu," Libby said to the African Canadian woman with braided hair circled on her head, bluish eyes and mahogany complexion who wore a long flannel grey and red checkered skirt with a turtleneck grey woolen sweater.

We shook hands and sat. Her office overlooked the city streets and avenues of expensive condominiums with long windows and balconies with flowering plants.

Nicola said, "The children across the street are being given a few days to acclimate to being inside buildings. We've already tested them for a battery of abilities - we did this in order to get them to come with us. We think but can't yet prove that the reason for the camps remaining fairly unimproved is because the captors eventually hoped to obtain passage to an island in Malaysia for the purpose of starting a tobacco plantation."

I didn't say that I thought the children were merely repositories for experimentation for adults who had contracted HIV. This was Libby's contact and whatever this team of child specialists derived would be Libby's palate.

"We've discovered they possess unusual stamina, abilities which most adults with training cannot compete with." She produced test results taken for endurance. "They can outlast you or I at running, at pulling weight, at holding their breath underwater, at diving, carrying burning wood from a campfire to a trench. It's like nothing you've ever seen."

"What can you give us on use of subjects as terrorist training?" Libby asked, I suspected more for my benefit than for hers.

"Well, they've been starved and it shows. They have presumeably witnessed the deaths of a handful of older teens," and laid out both samples of shots I had taken along with glossies surrendered by the police detectives. "They appear to think as a unit rather than to use individuals among them for leadership. And they do not respond to their birth names but call one another by numbers. There is One, Two, Three and so on, the oldest being Eleven, so it posits there were others in the original group some two years ago."

"Scary," I said, and removed my notepad. "Any correlation by number to places or things?"

"Yes," she answered, apparently pleased to have my interest. "One is a lookout. There was a place called One that they left approximately a month ago near Hanalei. Two is a runner and knows at least two of the captors. Three is a stick numeric code possibly for counting or for a type of occurence, we haven't had the opportunity to discern which. However we found evidence of the counting system inside the graves you photographed so we think this was a part of the brainwashing. Four is a girl who we think may be a bleeder but again, too little information, strictly conjecture. Her bones break easily suggesting reoccurring physical trauma. Is the bone splintering deliberately induced? Whereas this is not rare, in this group it is being seen as exceptional.

"The oldest in this group is Eleven. Does this account for the three who are dead? We won't know until we bring in the older group. Even if that is any time soon, we are still left with a disparity in continuity and have to ask ourselves why the gap between Seven, who is a mildly asphasiac male youth, and Eleven? And if Eleven is followed by teens who from the other group also were given similar names, what constituted the decision to separate the groups?"

I reviewed what I had written. "Any speculation as to what the inference is that is represented by Seven Eleven?"

"At the moment with nothing more to go on we think these are actual symbols for a rope ladder and a hoe and that these are activities the captors taught these children, specifically how to climb a rope ladder up these mountains or across distances between peaks for example and the act of gardening or uncovering earth."

"Interesting," but I didn't know what to make of it and apparently neither did she. If I delved further for the specific acts of terrorism which had condemned these children, perhaps I would identify other ways in which the language of the symbols mattered. "It seems almost to be an interpretive language for gravediggers."

Nicola eyed me appreciatively. "Yes, a sociologist said something quite similar. Of course to my eye I keep seeing the numbers 711 as signifying a chain link fence that one pulls across a walkway or a train at the end of the line."

"The end of a line," Libby said reflectively in her kitchen. "The tracks don't go further. They should've led to a lime salted pit and would've perhaps if the children died."

"It's too Kilgore for my tastes," I said.

"Oh well." She removed the lasagna dish from the oven. "A dozen articles will hit the front page tomorrow and in a week it'll be over. What time do you leave?"

"Tomorrow at three. I thought I'd take in some swimming and a boat ride on a glass bottomed boat."

"Tourist stuff." She crinkled her nose. "This is not exactly the article you came to write."

"It's okay. I wanted to fly to Lanai but they've closed it to public access again. I considered Molokai for a night but David wants me back. He's run out of staff to cover my desk."

"You'll be back. We'll stay in touch. You remember Harry?"

I smiled. Harry was the man who came for us in the boat when the Red Chinese pelted the border with mortar. He was a shrimp and carried a lantern that no one shot at as the boat slipped through the silky dark waters on its way to the mouth. "Yeah. I sometimes think of them and wonder if they are okay."

Her eyes watered. "I went with him to look for his son. We went on land into occupied Cambodia and were separated. A reporter from Britain flew me out."

The tears were dry. For her, emotion was a luxury even among close friends. I found myself thinking she had taken Kane to bed to put distance between us so I couldn't take much of her with me. It was the parting I think that clawed her the most.

"I love you, Libby. You're an incredible woman."

It was her turn to smile and she produced a lopsided grin fraught with barely acknowledged sorrow. "Avi, there was a time when I could've married you."

I knew what she meant. If we had not made it out of Nam. Or if in escaping we'd been cut off and thwarted in Malaysia.

Life takes the uninitiated in unforeseen circles which if one is lucky brings ever deepening understanding of irony and complication. The initiated are carried by their own colors of lavender, violet and mauve. Had I been younger, somewhere in between thirty-five and forty-six, had I been more selfish or more encumbered, I too could have plummeted into the burdens of lost children and lost adults. But I had come prepared and I left with only the weights of an article and the needs of friendship.

As the plane arced above the land and the sandy beach,

above the aqua blue crystalline waters and the gradual blue to sapphire ocean, I felt that knot that comes with recognizing one's mortality at the notion one could never arrive safely to the port of call. I had stopped wishing I were Libby when I finally understood the nature of her marriage. I stopped agonizing over my turning fifty-two when Quenan told me on the last night of my stay that her husband's father had wanted her to bind her feet but doing so would have robbed her of her ability to farm.

Somewhere between the effects of the Dramamine tablet I had chewed and the clearing of the peanut wrapper and soda water for a prelunch snack my thoughts returned to the child whose body had been laid to rest at the City of Refuge. I thought about the tragic waste of his young life and the brutality of the people who had kidnapped him, of their disregard for his life and of the grief his parents once they came to collect his body would finally be able to try to resolve. One did not get over the loss of a child; one just survived it and somehow endured.